BEST BONDAGE EROTICA 2

BEST BONDAGE EROTICA 2

Edited by

Alison Tyler

Published in the United States by Cleis Press Inc.,
P.O. Box 14697, San Francisco, California 94114.

Printed in the United States.
Cover design: Scott Idleman
Cover photograph: Roman Kaperski
Text design: Frank Wiedemann
Cleis Press logo art: Juana Alicia
First Edition.
10 9 8 7 6 5 4 3 2

"Fire and Ice" by Rachel Kramer Bussel appeared in *Ultimate Lesbian Erotica 2005* (Alyson Publications, 2004). "Jane's Bonds" by Shanna Germain appeared in *The Many Joys of Sex Toys* (Broadway, 2004). "Her Beautiful Long Black Overcoat" by Bill Noble appeared in *Naughty Spanking Stories from A to Z* (Pretty Things Press, 2004). "See Dick Deconstruct" by Ian Philips appeared in *Best Gay Erotica 1999* (Cleis Press, 1998), and *Best of the Best Gay Erotica* (Cleis Press, 2000). "All Tied Down" by Ayre Riley appeared in *MASTER/slave* (Venus Book Club, 2004).

To SAM

Do not consider painful what is good for you.

—EURIPIDES

Many of us spend our whole lives running from feeling with the mistaken belief that you cannot bear the pain. But you have already borne the pain. What you have not done is feel all you are beyond the pain.

—BARTHOLOMEW

Acknowledgments

I'm forever bound in gratitude to Violet Blue, Eliza Castle, Mike Ostrowski, Barbara Pizio, Thomas S. Roche, Kerri Sharp, Rachel Kramer Bussel, and of course the ever-remarkable Felice Newman and Frédérique Delacoste.

CONTENTS

Introduction

Alison Tyler

I've always been into bondage. I just didn't know it at first. Or, at least, I didn't have the vocabulary to explain the cravings that surged through me. I couldn't have discerned the letters B/D or S/M from the rest of the ABCs. Yet from the beginning, I understood there was something different about my desires. While friends fantasized about French-kissing the celebrities of their dreams, I imagined being tied up by the stars of mine. And the celebs we admired never seemed to overlap. The tittering teenyboppers in my high school postered their bedroom walls with pictures of pretty boys—Jon Bon Jovi. Sting. Simon Le Bon—while I yearned for men, men who looked like they wouldn't be put off by the things that turned me on. Older men. Rugged me. Dirty men. My giggling girlfriends nursed crushes on Tom Cruise circa *The Firm.* I kept it quiet that I would rather find myself bound tightly for Gene Hackman, star of the very same movie.

You see, from the start I wanted to be held in place, captured, made to stay still.

My first serious boyfriend understood what I required.

Maybe I was sending out silent signals. Maybe I just look like the sort of girl who needs a bit of old-fashioned discipline in her life. I didn't have to make the first move. He took charge from our very first date. When he kissed me outside my front door, he anchored me in place by gripping firmly on to my long, midnight-black ponytail and biting hard into my full bottom lip. When he fucked me, he held my slender wrists over my head, so that I couldn't go anywhere. And when we moved past those innocent first baby bondage steps, he used gleaming metal cuffs, his old leather belts, or diamond-patterned silk thrift-store ties that he owned for no other purpose than keeping me in my place. (He wasn't exactly a tie-wearing sort of guy.)

Even more important than the toys he owned were the words he possessed. He knew the magic of making me call him Sir or Daddy, as in "Yes, Sir, whatever you say, Sir." And "Sorry, Daddy. I didn't mean to be such a bad girl." He punished me for my endless infractions—and I misbehaved in order to win his wrath. We made a perfect team: kinky and connected.

He read me. He understood. Without me having to ask, he knew.

When we were out in public, he didn't need words to make me toe the line. He had bindings that kept me in my place and at his side, invisible bindings that others might not have been able to see—but I could. I could feel them as intensely as I could feel his strong hand grasped around my glossy, shoulder-length hair, or his ties tight on my teenage wrists, or his cold metal cuffs binding me to his bed.

The authors in this collection will bind you to their stories with invisible ties, as well. Rakelle Valencia's "Buckle Fucker" takes you right up onto the back of a bucking bronco before roping you down to a bed for just as powerful a session between the cheap motel sheets. In "Her Beautiful Long

Black Overcoat," *Clean Sheets* editor Bill Noble visits an S/M club in San Francisco with his girlfriend and her dominant Republican lover, where the tension couldn't be tighter or the scene more explosive. Elaine Miller gives a whole new meaning to being a team player in the lesbian three-way tale "Be a Good Sport." The extremely talented Marilyn Jaye Lewis's powerful foray into the mind of a cheating wife in "Dinner at Eight" will leave you as breathlessly lustful as the wine-swigging main character herself. And Tom Piccirilli's mesmerizing tale of two lonely singles in "It Ain't Always Easy" teaches several important lessons—including the fact that you should always know where you left the handcuff key before you begin to play!

From start to finish, these bondage-inspired stories are luscious, naughty, and infinitely sexy. And I promise you this: they'll definitely have you bound to your chair and begging for more.

Alison Tyler
San Francisco
May 2005

All Tied Down

Ayre Riley

"Let's try it, Gracie," Gabriel whispered to me, his face pressed against my long auburn hair, his strong arms holding me tight. "We can stop any time you want. We won't have to do anything more than that—"

He wanted to tie me down. Just tie me down and fuck me. No chains. No whips. Nothing scary. His voice was both patient and hesitant, as if he were scared that I might not agree, but he needn't have worried. I've always been into playing with new ideas. I had no problem with doing it outdoors, fucking in the back of his shiny black pickup truck after a rock concert at the Greek Amphitheater, going down on him on the aerial ride at the amusement park at the beach, the little blue metal car swinging and swaying with our raucous movements. And even though I'd never told him about my fantasies—well, deep down, I'd always wanted to play a little more kinky. Or a *lot* more kinky. Even if I never told *anyone*, I'd always had these urges that went unfulfilled by all of my past good-guy boyfriends.

"Are you game, Gracie?" Gabriel asked me, his arms

around my trim waist, pulling me even closer to his muscular body in a spoon embrace. "Are you, baby?"

I rolled out of his grip to look over at him, and I realized as I stared at his gentle, yearning expression that I've always been with the good guys. You know how some girls always go for the bad boys? The ones who treat them cruelly, who don't call when they say they will, who don't act like gentlemen in any manner of speaking? I've never fallen for that type. The Mickey Rourke type. The Colin Farrell type. Unlike many of my friends, I never saw the appeal in dating a guy who could only think about racing motorcycles and wearing well-worn leather. I never yearned for rough whiskers and whiskey breath. But in the back of my head, I always wondered, *did it take a bad boy to give me what I craved?* Would it take going in for that sort of sickly twisted relationship in order to get what I needed? I hoped not. That's all I could do—just hope.

I never mentioned my sexual daydreams to Gabriel. I liked him too much, and I was scared I'd frighten him off if he ever saw the real me, the one I carefully concealed from everyone else: parents, teachers, girlfriends. But now, *he* was the one bringing up the concept. He was the one saying that he wanted to tie me down. Just tie me down and fuck me. Nothing scary. So why not? Why would I say no to something that he promised would bring me great pleasure?

And he was right—it did.

Being tied to the mattress was divine. I lay in the center of the bed, my wrists over my head, my ankles spread wide apart. Gabriel used his own expensive work ties to fasten my trembling limbs, and when I turned my head I saw that for my wrists he'd chosen a tie I'd given him for the previous Valentine's Day: a navy blue one decorated with miniature crimson hearts. That made me smile and relax. Yes, we were dabbling in bondage, but this was my sweetheart, my one-and-only. Even when tying me down, he played nice.

He took a moment to look at me, and I could tell that he was admiring my naked form bound for his own personal pleasure. When he was ready, he climbed onto the bed and used his tongue to trace pretty pictures up and over my clit. He took his time, moving away from me when I was desperate for him to let me climax. Only giving in when he was good and ready.

But he didn't want to stop there.

"You liked that, right?" he asked, his sex-glazed mouth so close to my ear that his breath warmed my skin. "Didn't you, Gracie?"

I nodded, my whole body still alive and tingling with pleasure. "Yeah, I did." Being bound was even better than I'd pictured; better than I'd fantasized about alone, my fingers moving quickly and making their magic circles up and over my clit, up and over, until it happened. In my head, I hadn't understood the power of being powerless. Now, I was starting to figure everything out.

"So let's take things up a notch."

"Meaning?"

"You tell me, Gracie. What would that mean to you? What visions does that idea conjure up for you?"

I closed my eyes, trying to guess what he expected me to say, trying to read his fantasies solely from the way he was asking the question. What would a good boy like Gabriel fantasize about? What would an all-American guy like my sandy-haired boyfriend think was pushing the edge? Gabriel's a devoted son with an upstanding job. He's a man who's never once forgotten my birthday, or our anniversary, or any special occasion at all. He's even bought me gifts on St. Patrick's Day. What would *he* consider kinky? I was already tied down—and he had ravaged me without me being able to do anything about it. Not that I'd wanted to do anything about it. He'd started by kissing my lips, letting me return his passion beat for beat, and then he'd moved slowly down, working his way along my entire body until he had reached that place between my legs, the place so desperate to feel the wetness of his kisses, and—well, what could be better than that?

"Blindfold," he suggested, breaking into my thoughts. "A blindfold, Gracie?"

So, yeah, as soon as he said the word, I thought that I should have known to say it myself. I've spent many pleasurable hours imagining the appeal in the abandonment of a sense, picturing how it would feel not to know where he was going to go next, what he was going to do, when he was going to fuck me.

"Sure," I said, trying not to sound as excited as I really was. I didn't want to spoil the effort he'd put into creating this exotic encounter. Would he possibly think less of me if he knew that sometimes, just *sometimes*, I take one of my expensive silk scarves, the ones I wear when I go to out-of-town conventions, and blindfold myself before allowing myself to come? I close my eyes tightly under the slippery fabric and pretend that Gabriel is the one placing the blindfold over my eyes, that he is the one plunging my world into darkness.

"Really?" Gabriel asked.

"Yeah," I said slowly, "that would be okay."

I was still agreeing when he brought the purple velvet blindfold out of the dresser drawer and held it up for me to see before positioning it over my eyes and fastening the back beneath my heavy hair. I had only long enough to realize that he'd gone out and purchased this particular toy for our use, that he'd planned this event for me, that it wasn't in the least bit spontaneous—and then we started again, with Gabriel kissing me all over, alternating the places he paid attention to and the pressure of his kisses, so I had no concept of what to expect. His mouth was wet and open, and I shivered at every connection of that wet heat with my naked skin.

Then suddenly he moved over my body, reaching in the drawer again. After a moment, I felt something different, something which I recognized instantly as a feather, caressing and playfully tickling the bottoms of my feet, my inner thighs, working right up over my clit, which still hummed from my first orgasm of the night.

"You trust me, right?" he murmured. "Right, Gracie?"

Deep breath. Did I trust him? Yeah. Of course, I did. I nodded.

"Say it."

"I trust you, Gabriel."

"Mean it."

"I do," I said quickly. "I do trust you. Of course I do."

"Then confess to me—"

"What—" I stuttered. "What do you mean?" All at once, the fact that I couldn't see him made me feel off balance. This idea of being captured, a concept I had explored in my head for years, took on a deeper meaning. I couldn't see him with the blindfold in place. I couldn't get free without his assistance. What expression was on his face? Precisely how intently was he staring at me?

"Now, tell me the secrets you've been keeping."

My breath came faster now. I tested the binds with my wrists and my ankles, for some reason feeling intensely confined when before I'd only felt erotically captured. He brought that feather back into play, so that I was wildly squirming and laughing even as my mind scrambled desperately to figure out what he wanted me to say.

"I read your journal, Gracie," he said—the one to actually confess—"so I know. I know all about it, baby. So now you tell me."

Oh, Christ. Oh, Jesus. Oh, *fuck*.

"I know what you think about when you take that naughty little hand of yours and bring it between your legs late at night. I know you wait for me to fall asleep, listen for my breathing to go soft and heavy, and then the sticky sap starts to flow down your thighs as you crest the waves of those silent orgasms. I know everything. But I need you to tell me. I need to hear you say it."

So he *did* know. Knew more than I was willing to tell even myself. That what I wanted was this. But more than this. Far beyond this. What I wanted was for him to take control. Total control. Not to ask me anymore if this was okay, or if that was okay, but to just do it. To do everything. To do whatever he wanted to with me. Using me. Taking me. Forcing me. No more nice and sweet and gentle lovemaking for his pretty girlfriend. But real and hard and fast and raw. And I understood even more than that: before he started, I had to say it all out loud. Creating truth from fantasy. Making it all real.

"Say it," he insisted.

"I want—" but the words died right there.

"Say it, Gracie."

"I want to be yours."

"You are mine."

"More than that."

"Say it."

"I want you to do things to me."

He sighed. "Oh, yes, baby, I know." My request unleashed a torrent from him. As if he'd been waiting forever for me to say the words that would set his own fantasies free. "You want me to fuck you hard. Isn't that right? Harder than I do now. Harder than I've dared. You want me to take you doggy-style, my hand in your hair, holding you steady for my pace. You want me to slam you up against the wall and just fuck you, holding your wrists over your head, keeping you right where I want you. You want me to make you touch yourself when we're caught in traffic, right there in the car, where everyone can see you, if they'd only look. You want to *have* to do what I tell you. Is that right? You want me to make you do things."

I nodded.

"Is that right?" he said again, his voice more softly menacing than I'd ever heard it before.

"Yes, Sir," I managed to respond. "Yes, yes, yes."

"But what if you fail me?"

And now we were at the part of the fantasies that I'd written down quickly in my journal but refused to reread. The parts that gave me the most pleasure as well as the most shame.

"Then—" I started.

"Yes, Gracie? What, then?" His whisper was almost scaring me. A hiss. A demand for more information.

"Then I want you to punish me."

"Punish you how?"

I couldn't turn back now. I had it within my grasp to get everything I'd ever wanted. I had to come clean. I had to do exactly what Gabriel insisted. Confess. "I want you to spank me with your hand and your belt. With a Ping-Pong paddle. With whatever you need to use. A wooden spoon. A ruler. A hard-backed hairbrush. I want you to make my ass burn from the blows, and then I want you to stand me in the corner with my panties dangling around my ankles so I can think about how I might better please you in the future."

"What else?" Gabriel asked me. "What else should I do to you if you disobey me?"

I took a deep breath. "I want you to call me names, to slap my face, to use clothespins on me."

"Clothespins?"

"You know, on my nipples, and my pussy lips, and my clit—" Now, I was grateful for the blindfold, so I wouldn't have to see the look on his face. Would he leave? Was he disgusted with me? "I want you to make me beg and—"

"And—"

"I want you to make me cry—"

"Oh, Gracie. Who would have thought? Who would have thought that my good girl could be such a bad girl at heart?"

I didn't have an answer for that. I didn't have an answer for anything. I was waiting, my breath held, to see what he'd say next. To see how he'd deal with all I'd just confessed to. He'd read my fantasies, but could he handle them now that I'd said everything out loud? Now that I'd really come clean. Now that I'd confessed.

"Of course I will," my good-guy boyfriend said. "Anything you need, baby," my all-American man promised me. And I suddenly realized that maybe you don't need to date a rough-and-tumble guy in order to find a Master. You only need a kindred spirit. That maybe Gabriel was looking the whole time for someone like me, a good sort of girl, fine and upstanding, sweet and even-tempered, who wanted only to serve and obey and be disciplined for failing her Master.

And so here I am, exactly where I always wanted to be, all tied down and nowhere to go....

Dinner at Eight

Marilyn Jaye Lewis

Tonight I'll be at another dinner party with my husband on the Upper East Side. All of us dining in style together smug and safe, rich lousy white fucks. I'll wear the black DKNY cocktail dress, the Gucci high heels. I am getting so fucking clichéd, even I can't stand myself anymore. I need something concrete and decisive here, like a divorce. I need to do that. When am I going to get my shit together, exactly—when it hits the fan?

"Jesus, *Mami*, you amaze me," he says, breaking in on my never-ending pseudo-psychotherapy pep talk. "You're too much."

It's the wine that triggers this assessment of me again, my need to have a good bottle of red within arm's reach whenever I'm getting ready to get screwed. And right now I'm taking a bottle of very decent '94 *Gran Reserva* out of my oversized shoulder bag. The bag that now feels considerably lighter, minus the bottle of imported Spanish wine. I've brought the right wine for the occasion once again, even though we're in a very sleazy, pay-by-the-hour motel in some godforsaken concrete hellhole corner of Brooklyn and it's the middle of a bitingly cold December afternoon. There is *maybe* a trickle of heat in this room. I am so fucking freezing and in a matter of minutes, really, I'm going to be stark naked in here, all of my own volition.

"How are we supposed to open that?" he asks. "It has a cork."

I retrieve the handy corkscrew from my bag. "This is how," I say and I hand it to him. I'm smiling. I'm so fucking excited to be in this piece of shit room with him, alone. A roof and four walls all to ourselves for twenty-five dollars an hour. Hardly what you'd call paradise, but any place where I can get myself alone with him becomes paradise on some level. The fact that there's even a bed in here, crummy as it looks, is just icing on the cake.

He hands the corkscrew back to me. "I'm not too good at this," he explains. "You do it. I don't drink much in the way of wines that have corks in them, you know that."

I'm still smiling. Not in that patronizing way, I hope. Not that "isn't it cute how he's so coarse and from the street" way. I'm smiling because I love everything about him. It's always so refreshing. He would never last a minute at one of our dinner parties. I'm not sure how much that matters to me in the long run. For now, it matters not one iota. I couldn't care less if I attend one more stinking dinner party.

"How did you know about this place?" I ask, unscrewing the cork from the bottle.

"I grew up not far from here."

"Here?" I'm shocked but I try to hide it. "You grew up around *here?* Was it always this horrible?" I backpedal a little. That sounded insulting. "I mean, with this elevated subway and all, it seems so dark. Even in the middle of the day."

"It's shitty, I know. But I grew up here. This is the old hood." He examines the bed doubtfully before sitting down on it. The blanket is full of stains but it looks washed, at least. He's still dressed. "I always wondered what it was like in here, in this fuck-motel," he says. "It's been here since I was a little kid. For as long as I can remember, men were taking hookers in and out. It sucks in here, doesn't it?"

"It's not the most glamorous place we've ever come up with, but at least we can be together for an hour. Make love."

He grins sheepishly. "You make love, Mami. I fuck."

"Yes, you fuck," I agree easily. "I know you fuck." And it makes me so crazy when we fuck—and when we can't fuck, I continue on in my head. It makes me crazy when I can't be with you. I'm crazy about you, Ricky. You, as a man. Not just your cock up my ass for a few stolen moments or your incredible mouth on me, but all of you. I love you. I want to be with you forever.

But first I have to decide on that divorce, before I say anything like that out loud.

The wine is open, the cork is out. I set the bottle on the scarred hunk of wood that passes for a night table. I'm letting the wine breathe but I'm not going to tell him that. He makes fun of me. He couldn't care less about wine. Next to the bottle on the table there's a clock that actually works, methodically ticking away our precious fuck-minutes.

"Christ," I say. "Look at the time already." Forget about letting it breathe. I take a healthy swig of wine from the bottle. I begin to undress. It is absolutely frigid cold in this room.

"I think I can actually see my breath," he says at the same moment.

"It's not that bad."

He gets up and fiddles with the radiator to no avail while I strip out of everything. Everything but my shoes. I don't have any idea what's hiding deep in the fibers of this filthy carpeting, and I don't want to know. And I don't want my feet touching it, either.

"*Ooh mamacita*," he says, laughing. "You look freezing."

Stark naked except for a pair of killer high heels, I take another swig of wine from the bottle. I don't say anything now, I just let everything happen. I surrender to the rhythm that I know is coming because we've already done this so many times before. He knows it and I know it.

"What else have you got in your bag?" he asks, dragging it onto the bed now and rifling through it.

I'm standing next to the bed, shivering. I keep on drinking the wine. I feel pressured to make some serious progress with it since we're racing against the clock here. Every time he goes through that bag of mine, I feel a little invaded and defensive. It's not like I don't want him to go through my bag, or that he hasn't done it countless times, but I always feel exposed. My wallet comes out on the bed, my hairbrush—the "icky brush," he calls it, because I never clean it. There are so many strands of my long, dark hair tangled in its bristles. The greasy, well-used bottle of lube comes out next. The glistening silicone dick comes out, too; the one that always, without fail, goes up my ass and no place else. He usually sticks it up me early on in our trysts because he's going to want his cock in my ass eventually. I can't easily accommodate the size of his cock without a little help getting my hole open first.

At last the two items we both know he's really been looking for come out. The stocking. (He doesn't know it but when that stocking was new and part of a pair, it cost three times as much as the entire tab for our lunch earlier at the diner, tip included.) And the blindfold. The handy, light gray one that American Airlines was so kind to supply for me the last time I flew to London first-class—a sleeping mask, really. I seem to have no limit to my supply of handy airplane sleeping masks.

"Turn around," he says. And I do. My hands are already behind me, waiting for the nylon stocking to tie them together. Not too tight, but tight enough to feel the restraint will hold.

"Okay, turn back around," he says. And I do, my pussy already engorged. It happens that fast. Tie me up, even just a little bit, and I'm instantly a slick, sopping swollen ache down there between my legs. My clit is at eager attention under a perfectly trimmed thatch of pitch-black hair that's right at his eye level now. I imagine that he can smell me from where he's sitting, I'm already that aroused.

It would be so perfect if he moved his head just a little closer and put his tongue on my clit. Right on it. It would feel electrifying. But he puts the bottle of wine to his lips instead and takes a quick swallow.

"You want some?" he asks, holding the bottle up at me.

"Yes," I say.

He stands up next to me and helps me drink from the bottle. Then he puts it down. He retrieves the blindfold from the bed and slides it snugly over my eyes. It's a perfect world now. "Sit down," he says, helping me find the edge of the bed.

My soaking pussy meets the blanket and I wonder how many other slick cunts have wiped against it over the years. It doesn't matter. Right at this moment, I couldn't care less about anybody's slick cunt but my own. Now my acute sense of hearing is my lifeline to the entire world. I am only a waiting mouth, a clit, and two very eager holes. And for some reason, as the wine and hormones battle for supremacy in my veins, I feel absolutely alive. Following the mystery of this man is now my only goal.

I hear the zipper of his jeans come down. In a heartbeat, his warm balls are pressed against my lips.

"Christ, your face is cold," he says.

I don't answer. I kiss his balls. I lick them. When I feel his hands grab on to my hair and push my face closer, I lick his balls more ravenously, isolating one of them and sucking it into my mouth.

"*Ow*," he says. "Easy."

I go easy on it, but I feel like devouring him. His scent arouses me. The touch of his hands on my head, that element of being under his control, makes me feel insatiable for him.

He guides my mouth away from his balls and soon his cock is at my lips, the head pushing in, my lips parting, my mouth accepting the full length of him. All the way in and then all the way out, sliding slowly at first, rhythmically, until it begins to resemble fucking. His cock going in and out of my mouth, picking up speed. His cock filling up my dark world, becoming all that's in it. I'm moaning on that hard cock. I love the power of it filling my mouth. It's thrusting more urgently now. In and out. I keep moaning, it's uncontrollable, my delight. The spit collects at the corners of my mouth, drooling down now, onto my chin. I can't help it—my hands aren't free to wipe it away. His cock is a slippery mess of my spit as he fucks it in and out. I can feel his cock getting incredibly hard.

"I'm going to come," he says haltingly. "Let's stop for a minute."

He helps me to turn over, to find my bearings dead center on the bed. He helps me to lean forward, to go all the way down into the darkness, my weight resting on my shoulders, my knees spread and my ass in the air. The blanket is scratchy against my face, but it smells faintly of bleach. I'm relieved by that smell. I feel him slipping off my high heels. I am instantly more comfortable.

Nothing happens for a while; how long, I'm not sure. He's doing something but god only knows what.

I feel so fucking aroused in this position. Oblivious to everything in the sighted world. My hands tied tight enough to make me feel helpless, to feel at his mercy, to have to rely on my sense of trust. I'm hoping that whatever he has in mind for me won't be more than I can handle. I know him. Something will be going in my ass. It's just a question of what and when.

He's moving stuff around on the bed. Suddenly there's a sharp *thwack* sound in the air, simultaneous with a stinging smack on my ass.

"*Shit*," I screech. It was too unexpected and it really hurts.

"Clean your hairbrush already," he says. "It's disgusting."

I make a mental note to clean the "icky brush" or maybe to just buy a brand-new one. I'm waiting with a keen sense of anticipation, but there are no more smacks across my ass. The sting of that sole stroke of the brush is radiating across my cheek. If he wanted to hit me some more, I would be okay with it. If he wanted to spank me with that brush repeatedly, until my flesh was burning, until I was bawling like a little kid, I would be all right with that, too. I don't tell him that, I don't say anything at all, but in my secret heart I know it's true. He could push me much harder than he usually does and I would follow his lead without complaining. I might cry or whimper. I might beg him to show a little mercy, but I wouldn't complain. I would writhe in absolute ecstasy instead, I'm sure of it.

"Shit!" I cry out again, only this time it's because the lube he just squirted up my ass is icy cold. "Oh god," I'm moaning as I succumb to the anticipation of it, to the head of the silicone dildo that's suddenly sliding into my ass. "Yes," I stutter. Christ, it feels good. And now *this* is my whole world, the focus of all my lust: the insertion of the slick dick into my ass, pushing me open easily, finding its way up my depths and filling me with cold and that insane pressure of fullness.

Usually he slides the dick in up to its fake balls and just lets it sit there in my ass, taking his time with me, going about his business. But now we are paying by the hour and I'm a long way from home. Today, we're pressed for time. He uses that silicone dick for what it was made to do. He fucks my ass with it. But the motion is too sudden. He's a little too thorough with that fake dick, a little too rough. I cry out, but it doesn't matter. He doesn't stop.

I won't admit it to him, or to anyone else on earth, but I love this very thing, when I can't differentiate between pleasurable ass-fucking and ass-fucking that is way too rough. I'm crying now, I'm begging for him to stop, but my ass is arching up higher, helping the dildo get in deep.

I'm crying but the words that are coming out of my mouth are, "Fuck me, Enrique, fuck me."

In a mere moment, the dildo is out and he's between my legs on the bed, mounting me, my ass in his steady grip as he aims his cock at my slicked-up hole and pushes it in.

But now this is really too much. I can't handle this. His cock feels huge and my hole isn't ready for this size of intrusion. "Ricky, no," I'm begging. "No, it hurts."

But his slick cock is taking over my hole, forcing it to fit his generous proportions. I know I can take it, I can open for him. I can take him balls deep. "Shit," I'm crying. "Shit, it hurts."

And then just as suddenly as it was intrusive, his furious, relentless cock-rhythm has opened me completely. It becomes a smooth ride, a heavenly connection of slick force and speed. I wish there were more of him to fill me. I want to take him in me as deep as anything can get.

"How you doing, Mami?" he calls down from the darkness.

"Good," I cry distractedly into the blanket. "I'm good."

"You ready for *Papi* to come?"

"Yeah," I say, "I'm ready for Papi to come."

"Where do you want it? Where should Papi come?"

"Up my ass, you can come up my ass." But I can't tell if he's wearing a rubber or not. This could be the real deal; if he's riding me bareback and he comes up my ass—how well do I really know him? How well do we really know anyone, I wonder? Fleeting visions of my husband surface in my head. He's supposedly hard at work in some lush office on Wall Street—who's *he* fucking now and is *he* wearing a rubber?

"You want me to come in your ass, Mami?"

"Yes, yes, I want you to. No, no, wait," I say, changing my mind.

He pulls his cock out of me abruptly. He pushes me down and then turns me over on the bed. Now all my weight is on my tied hands and he's on top of me.

"You rich white ladies always want to flirt with fire. Why is that, Mami?"

His cock is still rock hard and it's planted between our bellies, slippery and thick. He kisses my mouth. "You're not answering me," he says. "Can I come in your mouth?"

My world is still a dark, sightless place, but it's filled with such exquisite sensations. "Yes," I say, out of breath. "Come in my mouth."

I feel him shift his weight over me. I feel the head of his cock at my parted lips. The terrible taste of latex smothered in lube is instantly overpowering and he laughs. He's wearing a rubber. "Surprise," he says. "Yummy, isn't it?"

And then he's off me. For a moment, I'm lying there, panting, listening. What is he doing now? It sounds like he's slicking his dick with more lube.

Then he's back between my legs, his hands gripping my ankles, lifting them up, pushing them higher, lifting my ass off the bed. The pressure of my own weight is finally off my tied hands, but my knees are practically to my shoulders now. It's not very comfortable.

With little effort, he works his cock back in my ass and with ease my hole opens to take it balls deep again. God it feels good to get filled up with him. He fucks me for all he's worth now. As much as I liked the fantasy of feeling his spunk seep out of my hole later tonight at that dinner party, I know this is the better way. I don't know him at all, really. I don't know who he's been in his life, or who he's been with. But I want to know his secrets, I really do.

"Enrique," I cry quietly. My face is buried in his muscular chest as he fucks me.

"Yes, Mami?"

I want to say: I love you, tell me who you are. I want to know who you are. But instead, I say, "Fuck me, fuck my ass, Papi."

"Don't you worry, Boo, that's just what I'm doing."

Then just when it feels like my hole is stretched raw and can't take another minute more of his relentless pumping, his entire body goes rigid. His heavy weight is smothering me. I feel crushed, but I know he's coming. My ears are filled with the sounds of his consuming lust. The whole dark room takes on the sound of his urgency. His hips jerk against my hole in quick, hard thrusts. And then he becomes dead weight, falling on me.

"Jesus," he says, catching his breath.

I'm buried, motionless, impaled underneath his two-hundred-pound frame.

When he pulls his dick out of me, he says, "Was that good for you, Mami?"

I say yes.

"I think I know what Mami needs now." He helps me to sit up on the bed and then the wine bottle is at my lips. I take a couple swallows. "Let's clean you up," he says. "Our hour is almost up."

I can feel him sliding my high heels back on my feet. With his body off me now the room is once again freezing. I'm getting my bearings but the world is still dark.

He leads me across the room. I follow in halting steps. My legs are aching. The room feels even colder than it did before. My high heels hit porcelain tiles. We're in the bathroom. He's switched on the light. I can tell this because there's a sudden slight buzzing overhead from some kind of an electric fixture. The sink water is running.

"Sit down, Mami," he says, guiding me onto the toilet. It's ice cold.

"Jesus!" I cry out.

He chooses that moment to slip the blindfold off me. Immediately my eyes fill with the sight of his handsome Latino face, so full of warmth, of secrets, of hesitant compassion. I see now that the bathroom is tiny, garishly lit by one faintly flickering fluorescent tube. The walls are covered with graffiti. The shower curtain is torn and hanging uselessly on the shower rod from a half-dozen rusty rings.

He reaches behind me to untie my hands. It feels funny to be free. To suddenly have full use of my arms, my hands.

The towels the motel provides are barely large enough to dry a person's face. But that's okay, it's too damn freezing to risk taking an actual shower.

"Here," he says, handing me a soaking washrag. "Use this."

Thank god it's hot. I clean myself off with it.

"You're going to walk me to the train, right?"

"I'll ride all the way home with you," he says.

I'm relieved to hear it. We're in the middle of a concrete jungle of nowhere and frankly I'm not all that sure about how to get home from here. But more than that, I'm happy to have some additional stolen moments with him, even though we'll be out in broad daylight, on a public subway train. I'll have to be careful about being seen. "But that's so far out of your way," I protest, if only to be polite.

"That's okay," he insists. "I don't have to be anywhere. There's nobody waiting to take me to some cracker dinner party."

There's a tone in his voice that's accusing. I take it for the little slap of reality that it's meant to be. I'm going to a fancy dinner party. He lives in a rundown rooming house.

"Thank you, Enrique," I say, hoping that at least the

expression on my face can tell him I love him, that he isn't just an afternoon fuck, but that I still need time to figure it all out. After all, I'd be giving up everything, not just dinner parties....

"It's okay, Mami," he says. "You don't need to thank me. The pleasure is always mine."

But that is so far from the truth. The pleasure is mine, too. One of these days, I'll tell him that—as soon as I know it for sure.

Be a Good Sport

Elaine Miller

"You fucked up," I hissed to her as I pulled off my cleats and stuck them in my bag.

"Whatever," Erin said dismissively, bending to pull on her engineer boots. "We won. Let it go, Darcy. Everyone else has."

"Are you kidding? I was wide open! You saw me on the wing; I was totally clear!" Frustration bubbled up, robbing me of self-possession. "You could have made a perfect pass to me, but you want the whole pitch to yourself, don't you? You want to make the goal and be the hero. I'm on your team, but you don't want to share the game with me."

"Whoa, girl. Chill," said Erin. She passed her fingers through her flattop and rubbed the short hairs on the back of her head meditatively. "There's enough play to go around. The girls look at you too, you know. They should; you kinda look like me."

As I sat, mouth open in outrage, she tossed the last of her gear in her bag, picked it up, and walked off with an easy, long-legged stride. Even the fit of her biker's leather jacket across her strong shoulders looked insolent.

God, she pissed me off.

At home after dinner that day, I refused to think about Erin. I was busy getting ready for tonight's playdate with Miss Sheila Crof—the femme top so hot that me and every other butch bottom in town would walk a mile barefoot through snow to stand in her garbage. I checked on the final spit-shine of my boots. Sheila had promised me "something special" tonight. I wasn't going to fuck that up for anything.

Despite oodles of emailed negotiations over the last month, I'd only had one date with her—a briskly impersonal and devastatingly effective flogging at a public play party. Sheila's feline smile and the swish of her long red hair were the things I remembered most, other than the high that lasted—I swear—a week.

Sheila's smile, though cocky, was not infuriating the way Erin's was. Damn Erin! What the hell was the matter with her!

So that's how I find myself here, ringing Sheila's doorbell. She takes so long to answer the door that I need to dry my sweaty palms on my jeans twice, and then I hear a tick-tick of high heels on tiles from inside, and the door swings open wide.

One look at her, and I break into a fresh queasy sweat. She's got on shiny black rubber underwear, and she's wearing this thing on the top that must be more about engineering than tailoring, because her boobs are perched impossibly high and rounded. There are these long stockings, and her shoes are all black, sleek and spikey. I should know. I'm looking mostly at her feet now because I'm way too scared to look at her face and see the smile I know is there.

"Come in," she says, sounding amused, and oh god I'm frozen on her doorstep, I'm never going to be able to move unless it's to run in my heavy black boots all the way back to the bus stop. Then she turns away from the door, and her tiny rubber hot pants aren't covering her goddamn *ass* even a little and somehow I'm following her, would follow her anywhere.

"Close and lock the door behind you," she throws over her shoulder as she walks down the hall, *tick tick tick*. I have to backtrack a few steps, having, in my gobsmacked state, left the door wide open. Then I hurry after her.

She's standing in the hall by a closed door, holding cuffs and a collar. My knees start to bend of their own accord as soon as I see her standing there like my friggin' slickest wet dream, but she hasn't ordered me to kneel, so I simply stop and drink in the sight of her. "I promised you something interesting, Darcy. I'd like to do some...ah...complex bondage scenes." Sheila pauses. "With another bottom. She's here already. There'll be pain as well as bondage. You up for it?"

Now I could have sworn she promised something "special," not "interesting," and there's a world of difference between the two terms. But a gentlebutch doesn't quibble with a lady. What the heck. "Yes, ma'am." says I, all lamb-to-the-slaughter willingness.

"Excellent. Your safeword is pronounced *safeword*. Suits?"

I assent, a bit dry-mouthed. Sheila directs me to remove my clothes, except my boxers—how did she know I'd be wearing boxers? I hasten to strip, and then stand as she buckles the wrist cuffs and collar on. She snaps the cuffs together in front of me while I'm still dizzy with the feel of cool leather encircling my throat, then opens the door and pushes me on ahead, her hand on my shoulder.

The room is large, warm, softly lit, and contains what must be every piece of dungeon furniture ever invented. Three steps in, and I balk like a horse confronted by a rattlesnake. Un*befucking*lievable.

Erin, sporting nothing but a ball gag, a jockstrap, and cuffs and collar similar to mine, is standing stretched up against the far wall, her arms bound above her head and attached to the wall. She's been watching the door, and her eyes widen as she recognizes me.

Sheila gives me the tiniest shove and to my horror I keep walking, my mind racing so fast that my body is numb. We walk straight toward Erin, and just as I'm about to turn and run out the door, Sheila lifts my bound arms high with surprising strength, and slips the cuff connector into a carabiner clip attached to the wall. She eyes the two of us hanging side by side, with a quirk at the corner of her mouth, and turns and walks away.

Our eyes, on automatic, follow her perky, mocking ass-cheeks for a second, then I turn to Erin, outraged. "Is this your idea of a sick joke?" I hiss, as quietly as possible.

Erin's eyes grow even larger over her gag, and she shakes her head no.

"C'mon, you asshole, you found out who I was seeing tonight, and decided to horn in on it!" I'm yelling *sotto voce*, which I hadn't realized was possible.

Erin's eyebrows knit in annoyance, and she grunts at me emphatically through the gag, just as Sheila reappears tugging an honest-to-god locker-room bench, about six feet in length, into the center of the room. It's been modified slightly, and the modifications make merry clanking noises as the bench is moved. You could hitch an entire soccer team to the hardware on this bench. "Getting along well now, boys?" she says cheerily. "I don't hear any safewords, do I?"

We direct identical outraged glares at her. As mute as Erin for the moment, I press my lips together and shake my head. No way am I going to safeword in front of Erin, or because of her. I'll go through with this even if it kills me.

She unclips us both from the wall carabiners and turns to pick up some lengths of soft-looking rope. "Drop your underwear," she says in a voice like warm honey. Neither Erin nor I hesitate to obey, but we utterly refuse to look at each other.

Sheila obviously knows what's she's doing, because she doesn't hesitate as she pulls me over and directs me to sit on the end of the low bench. "No, Darcy, not like that. Sit astride, knees bent and feet tucked under, with your ass at the end. Face the empty length of it," she directs. "Yeah, back even further—like you're riding a horse and are about to fall off its butt."

I don't know why, but she finds this funny and giggles about cowboys to herself as she binds my knees to bolts placed just under the bench top, and then, pulling my arms straight down at my sides, clips my wrist cuffs to the bench bolts nearest my hips.

Erin, doing a creditable Old Stone Face, is led over and placed standing astraddle the bench, facing me. "Erin, boy, move forward a little," directs Sheila. "Stand over Darcy's knees. Mmm. Shuffle forward about five inches. Okay, right there."

The muscles in Erin's jaw flex around her ball gag as she pretends mightily that I'm not in the room, and the muscles in her long thighs flex as she strives to achieve a stance so wide she isn't touching me in any way. Sheila solves this recalcitrance with a few loops of rope and a couple of brisk tugs, harnessing Erin's calves firmly to each of my legs just above the knee. I can't decide how I feel about this, and I concentrate on not staring at Erin's tits, which are small, firm, and directly in front of my face.

Erin's wrists are bound behind her head and anchored there with a quick twist of rope in a figure eight around her shoulders. With her arms up and elbows bent like that, she looks like a caricature of leisure, like she's in her favorite lawn chair. Then Sheila picks up a tangle of nasty-looking clamps and fishing line, and after a few preparatory smacks of Erin's shoulder blades, places the clamps along her back. Erin grimaces and blows air through her nose at each pinch. Sheila stops every so often to check in with her, stroking her skin as she does, the way you'd gentle a horse, and when she's done, pushes the trailing fishing lines through a pulley in the ceiling, leaving the ends hanging limply.

Of course my turn is next, and I get to feel firsthand what Erin just experienced. Ow. Ow. Each clamp chomps ferociously into the skin across my back, and the fishing lines attached to them tickle maddeningly, trailing across my skin. With a whisper from Sheila I lean back slowly into midair, holding myself up with the tension in my belly muscles, until my upper body is in a perfect horizontal line with my thighs. She gathers up the lines to my clamps. I wonder what she is going to attach them to—but Sheila, who must have been a Girl Scout, is prepared with a crossed set of dumbbells of the hefty variety, which she kicks into position on the floor under me, and wastes no time in pulling the lines taut and securing them.

To ease the strain on my stomach muscles I allow my upper body to droop back toward the floor, and she flashes me a dangerous look. "Slumping already?"

I take that as a hint, and haul myself quiveringly horizontal. Sheila casually grabs for Erin's bound arms and pulls her into a bent-over position that leaves her hovering over me in a mockery of a courtly bow. She sucks hard on her gag, holding in the sudden rush of drool—a courtesy I appreciate beyond measure. There's a tiny rattle of chains, and then my right nipple explodes in pain. I sneak a glance, and groan. It's a butterfly clamp—the kind that grips harder the more you pull. Like the standard pair of clamps, these are joined by a slim chain, but instead of attaching the second butterfly clamp to my nipple, Sheila uses it to painfully compress Erin's left nipple. A second's work strings another set of clamps between Erin's right and my left tit, and she and I have become painfully conjoined twins.

Sheila then enjoys herself far too much as she adjusts our various chain and fishing-line tensions until even a slight movement up or down for either of us tugs at the clamps, then she ties off Erin's clamps at the ceiling pulley with an air of completion. She takes a good look into our tense, somewhat bug-eyed faces, then unbuckles and whisks away the ball gag with a final desperate slurp from Erin. Sheila walks away with a final comment: "You boys behave yourselves, now."

The click of the door closing behind her sounds very final, and the silence that follows is what the literary types like to describe as pregnant. For a while Erin and I stare over each other's shoulders as if we're in an elevator—an elevator where we're naked, straining to keep our upper bodies horizontal, and clamped together at the nipples. So the analogy breaks down, and so does Erin, who speaks first.

"I can't believe you thought I was doing this just to piss you off...."

"How could I not think? Everything you *do* pisses me off. You always like to be right in the middle of..." Both our voices are a bit strained from the discomfort of holding our positions, and from the clamps, but I find myself needing to either talk or bite her.

"Hey. You think I asked to be here?" There's a pause as Erin reflects on the absurdity of her statement. "Well okay, I did ask for this playdate. But *not*—I repeat —*not* with *you*."

My pride is stung. "Whoa, Mr. Undue Emphasis. What in hell's wrong with me?"

"This is gonna be *so* much fun," says Sheila brightly, as she swings the door open so suddenly that someone more cynical than I might suspect she's been standing just on the other side of it. We both fall silent, watching her warily. She dumps a small pile of toys on the bench behind Erin, then selects a long, wicked-looking leather strap, which she flexes meditatively for a few heartbeats, then brings down in a fast, decisive arc across Erin's exposed ass.

Erin starts violently upward, which yanks the chains between our nipples and sends a searing pain through my tits as the clamps bite hard. I lurch upward to lessen the pull, and as the clamps across my shoulders nip at me, I bite back a squeak and glare at Erin as if it's her fault. She's doing her own grimacing, having bent forward again rather suddenly to relieve the tension on her nipples. I can see the fishing line attaching her to the ceiling vibrating tautly, so I'm guessing she's had the one-two pinch as well.

Sheila smiles beatifically. She's making happy little humming sounds now, and swinging the strap at Erin's ass in long, slow, lazy blows. The first few, Erin jerks hard, making us both do the marionette-dance of pain, but then she settles into the rhythm of the strap, and stands steady, staring down at me with a challenging gaze.

I stare back, grunting a little with the effort of holding my body out straight with only my belly muscles, almost wishing that I could feel the strap, to prove to snotty Erin that I can take it too. Then I deeply regret the thought as Sheila speaks. "Poor Darcy, I've been neglecting you!"

She drops the strap and goes behind my head to fiddle with something in a cupboard. I can't see her, but Erin can, and she breaks out into a grin, which I know damn well does not bode well for me.

Sheila reappears wearing a well-lubed nitrile glove. Instantly, the word *safeword* trembles on my lips, then dies away unsaid. I can't chicken out now; I'd never live it down. Instead I feel a blush burn my ears and I avoid Erin's mocking gaze as Sheila sits on the bench directly behind her, scoots herself into a comfy lower position with the ease of a born mechanic, and reaching between Erin's legs and mine, slides her slippery fingers up inside me without even a pause to get acquainted. Embarrassingly, I realize she didn't need that lube, not really.

So I'm not saying that I haven't been dreaming for weeks about Sheila fucking me, that I haven't been jerking off to fantasies of her demanding fist inside me as I scream and scream and beg her to keep fucking me. But this is *not* how I'd seen it in my horny little mind's eye, not with Erin grinning down at me, not with the clamps on my tits and my back burning and tugging as I teeter back and forth from the horizontal with my abs gone all trembly from effort.

I refuse to cry out, to moan, to show any reaction. I can take anything, even this. I press my lips together, determined not to be my usual loud fuck-me-harder self. Then Sheila's slow stroking fingers find my G-spot, and a little grunty sex moan escapes me. Furious, I clam up again, and concentrate on how much I hate Erin's supercilious look. I'll just refuse to feel Sheila's slowly thrusting fingers moving faster, bumping my G-spot with a delicious firm stroke. I won't feel a thing. I won't give them—either of them—anything.

But somehow I'm having a hard time concentrating on keeping my upper body still, and I start to dip a bit, rhythmically, yanking on my own tits and Erin's, too. Serves her right. But that steady yanking on my tits is kind of my undoing; I've always had a hair-trigger and now I'm starting to make a little horrified groany noise between my clenched teeth, because I'm already feeling the heat build up. I'm just hoping Sheila's not gonna touch my clit, because if she makes me come like this I'll die of embarrassment.

She's fucking me pretty roughly now with what feels like four stiff fingers, having been welcomed in fast by my treacherous cunt, and then—oh, just my luck— she moves her slippery gloved thumb into a position where it grazes my clit with each stroke. In moments I don't care that I can't see anything but Erin's smugly grinning face, and something in me pulls in tighter and tighter, until it explodes outward and obliterates my thoughts. I yell myself hoarse as I come so hard

I think I might turn inside out. Still blindly coming, I howl again as my carefully horizontal position collapses, my head suddenly bonks the floor behind me and my nipples feel like they'll tear off. Then I shriek again, running out of air, half the clips wrenching free of my back as I rebound upward, frantic to save my nipples.

When I can see again in the explosion's aftermath, Erin's face above me is white and clenched and she's swearing a streak as Sheila, now ungloved, resets the clamps on her shoulders and strings her back up in the now familiar position. Then it's my turn to grimace and swear as she ducks underneath my back to reset those clamps over sore and abraded skin, although the continued happy throbbing of my traitorous clit takes some of the edge off.

Both Erin and I are sweating freely, our muscles straining as we strive to balance in our awkward poses. Sheila looks indecently happy, and is still humming. She disappears somewhere behind my head again, while Erin hisses at me, "That hurt, you bastard. You nearly pulled my fucking nipples off."

"Hey, I'm sorry, okay? I couldn't help it." I start to think about ways I could kill myself painlessly before the next soccer practice with Erin.

"You couldn't help it? That's a laugh." She glances over me at whatever Sheila's doing and then grins at me mockingly. "Looks like you'll have a chance to redeem yourself. I think you're going again."

Sheila appears, regloved carrying the lube bottle and a bright red, fairly hefty-looking butt plug. My sphincter snaps shut at the very sight of it. She seats herself on the bench behind us again, and I can't stand to look at Erin's mocking grin while my ass gets invaded, so I just close my eyes and clench my teeth and wait. And wait.

And suddenly my nipples get plucked upward and my eyes fly open and Erin's quivering there, face full of disbelief. I hear

Sheila's light and tinkling laugh, along with the breathy splutter of a lube bottle being squeezed, and I understand. And she takes her time about it too, working that big ol' plug into Erin's ass slowly, with lots of back and forth movement and salacious verbal encouragement. Erin's rocking body pulls a bit on my nipples, but I don't mind, as it's no longer *my* eyes that are closed in horror.

For the first time, I kinda feel sorry for Erin. Only a little sorry, mind you. But maybe this means dying from embarrassment will not be necessary.

With a last giggle from Sheila and a reluctant-sounding "Ungh" from Erin, it appears the deed's been accomplished. Sheila's obviously in a celebratory mood, because she drops her gloves, picks up a slim whip and spins it experimentally. Looking at its delicacy, I'm feeling optimistic until she actually starts using it on us. Light enough to be used on almost any part of our bodies, its heavily-oiled bootlace tails sting so much neither of us can keep still.

My world soon becomes a blur of struggling to remain more or less in position, belly aching with effort, the clamps burning behind and before, and always the whip, like a merciless insect, landing and biting my skin—or landing unfelt by me and followed by a painful jerk to my tits as Erin twists and swears. My perceptions are starting to whirl, and at first my only anchor is Sheila's warm, throaty voice as she describes to us exactly what handsome, brave boys we are, and how wet we're making her.

I find my eyes locked with Erin's now, as we watch each tiny struggle show on the other's face, the sudden pain of the lash, the constant ache of muscles holding us in strained positions, the slight humiliation of bouncing in painful jolts back and forth between us like a little perpetual motion machine.

Sheila lands a particularly whistling stroke across my thighs, and Erin's eyes flash at me as I struggle to cope with the searing pain without ripping our nipples off. "You can do it," she mutters, so softly, then sips air frantically as she gets her own whistler across the backs of her thighs. Although she grimaces ferociously, she makes it without yanking on our tits, and I nod at her encouragingly, appreciative of her ability to take it.

Three strokes crash across my thighs—hard ones—and I have to tense every muscle until my ears roar, but I've got something to live up to, now, and Erin smiles and mouths "Thanks, Buddy," when I make it through.

"Twelve more like that each, my sweet boys," says Sheila as my thighs explode in pain once more, and as I struggle to remain still, to take the lash, Erin's face twists as she gets hers, and then me again. We're twisting and jerking at our chains more now, not so controlled. I twist a bit too hard, and we both gasp at the pain in our nipples, and I mutter "Fuck, man, I'm sorry," and she says in a tight voice, "S'okay, it's hard..." and when the whip whistles through the air this time her eyes go wide and fresh sweat beads her forehead.

Soon it's hard to tell when I'm hit or when she's being hit—each blow runs through us both with a rattle of chains and a little tearing feeling from the clamp's teeth. But now we're staring at each other, willing each other to take it without moving, and acknowledging each other's efforts, and it makes it easier, somehow, than any other beating I've had...despite all the things that make it harder.

"Twenty-three...twenty-four... That's it, boys. You've done just perfectly." Sheila tosses the whip to the floor with a sigh. "That was really fucking hot. But I'm not feeling quite...done. Boys, will you do something else for me?"

We're still staring into each other's faces, panting still, and trembling. But we must be insane, because our "Yes, ma'am" comes out in unison.

"Good. Darcy, stick out your tongue."

As I comply, somewhat startled, Sheila throws a leg over

my head, and stands astraddle, legs thrown really wide apart. Looking up, I note that her black latex panties are pulled so tight over her cunt I can see her labia clearly and perfectly outlined.

I only get a second's look, though, because Sheila grabs Erin's hair and pulls her up sharply, causing a chain reaction of nipple pain that brings my whole upper body up past the horizontal with a pained grunt. I fetch up with my face pressed into the heat of her latex, my mouth open. As a few of the clamps on my back slide off, increasing the bite and tension of the few left, I groan loudly, little cartoon stars of pain shooting about under my squished-closed eyelids.

Sheila hums happily and rubs her latex-covered crotch on my mouth. My tongue obediently out and rigid, I can feel a little hard spot that must be her clit, because she's shoving it at me over and over. The fire in my belly muscles is having a contest with the fire in my nipples, and the burn of the clips across my back is coming in a very distant third. Every time my belly muscles fail and I droop a bit, I gasp for air, and Erin and I both groan at the increased tension on our nipples. It seems like everything I've seen tonight has been framed by somebody's thighs, and in this case I can see Sheila's hand working busily at Erin's clit. Then I can't stand the pull on my nipples, I tense my aching belly again, and the taste of latex fills my mouth as Sheila continues grinding her cunt on my face.

Surrounded in girl-flesh, I can't see a thing. Erin's leg muscles are not so much trembling as oscillating, and I'm wondering if she's gonna fall over on me or what, when suddenly her leg muscles go rock hard and she hisses a long intake of breath. Suddenly I know exactly what's gonna happen and I have just enough time to think "Oh no!" before Erin, with a hoarse cry, comes in a very big way. My nipples suddenly explode with pain, and as I fall backward with a shriek, I see

Erin standing bolt upright, eyes closed, face red and hips a-jerking on Sheila's probing fingers.

I can still hear squealing and realize it's me. I feel a kind of despair as I realize that the nipple clamps have popped right off Erin's nipples but, although shifted, they're *still attached to mine*, and Sheila reaches down left-handed, grabs the chains in one white-knuckled fist and hauls me back up to her spit-slick latex-covered cunt, mashing herself onto my face without care or regard for the feelings in my stretched-tight nipples or my need to breathe in instead of simply screaming out.

But I suppose my bubbling cries help matters along for her, because moments later she comes so hard she pulls those fucking clamps right off, and follows my face to the floor, going down on one knee as she works her latex-covered clit against my somehow still-yelling mouth, getting the last juicy growling seconds out of her orgasm. I almost pass out then, with some remote part of me marveling at how my tits hurt so bad that I don't care if I'm suffocating.

Then I'm feeling a rush of sweet air cooling my sweat- and spit-covered face as I slump, curved backward with my head touching the floor. I barely notice as Sheila, panting, carefully but quickly releases the clamps on my back. Each one is a small white-hot flash of pain. She pats me on my shoulder in an absurdly comforting gesture, releases Erin similarly, then pulls expertly at our various knots until our ropes are loose enough that we can complete the job of shaking them off.

My knees and hands released, I slither to the floor completely, and lie there, stunned. Sheila kicks off her shoes and sprawls on the floor beside me with a sigh, and Erin collapses along the bench like a lion in an Acacia tree, limbs dangling on the floor.

"At ease, soldiers," says Sheila dreamily to the ceiling.

"Holy goddamn fucking holy shit, Sheila!" says Erin, all muffled with her face smooshed into the bench.

For some reason this strikes me as absurdly funny, and I laugh until tears run into my ears and the room goes all wobbly. When I get myself under control and look up, Sheila's regarding me with kind and knowing eyes, while my brother-in-arms reaches out with a smile and smacks me on the leg. "Well, we lived through it," she says.

Later, as we put on our boots at the door, Erin offers me a lift home. I accept. As we walk down the driveway, she turns to me and says, "Hey, man, maybe you could come over and help me fix my TV."

"Huh?" I look sharply at Erin, but her face is serious. "Fix your TV? What in hell's wrong with it?"

"Well," she says, patting my aching gut and exhibiting a sudden gleeful grin, "I'm having problems with my horizontal hold."

I chase Erin the rest of the way to her car.

Jane's Bonds

Shanna Germain

It comes to her by mistake. Although it's her address on the plain brown envelope, it is someone else's name; perhaps the house's previous owner. She and Derek have lived here for almost five years, but they still get mail for the people that owned the house before them, people they've never met. She's about to stick the envelope back in the mailbox with a PLEASE FORWARD notice on it, when something below the name catches her eye: OR CURRENT RESIDENT. Oh, that's me, she thinks. It looks like junk mail of some sort, but she opens it anyway.

Inside the envelope is a purple catalog, offering "sexual satisfaction for women." She lies down on the bed and starts flipping through it—she's never seen so many women-oriented sex toys in her life. Sure, she's been to Fanta-She's-R-Us downtown (once even with Derek) but it always seemed like all the products were geared toward men—videos that offered nothing more than fake boobs and way-ugly men grunting, those ridiculous-looking fake mouths, rows and rows of cock rings.

But in this catalog (which, she realizes with little surprise, is from a woman-owned company), there are tons of toys for women—cool tie-dyed dildos in pink and purple, lipstick-shaped vibrators, even videos directed by women. She flips toward the back and there, tucked away on the last page, is a toy that catches her eye: two purple cuffs lined with fake fur.

She traces her hand along the page, imagining the cuffs' fur-lined softness against her skin. She's never used toys like these, but she's thought of it often, when Derek sometimes takes her hands and presses them to the bed during sex. She wonders if he'd go for it—probably not. Her husband's a wonderful man, but is still sometimes stuck in his religious upbringing, feeling guilty for anything outside of the missionary position. He's grown a lot since they met (getting him to go to Fanta-She's-R-Us was a big one) but still, he balks at things that are outside the mainstream (going to a strip club together for instance) and she never wants to push him too far or too fast. Still, she sighs as she runs her hand over the cuffs on the page, a few toys would be nice.

She reads the description: "Soft and delicate, yet tough in all the right ways, these fur- and silk-lined bonds are sure to please." And there's even a matching blindfold. She wonders if she should just buy them, let Derek find them somewhere in the house and act surprised. Or maybe she should put them on her wish list—her thirtieth birthday is coming up.

An image pops into her head of opening a gift like this, late at night, after a good meal and a glass of wine. Perhaps she's already opened her other gifts, and they're cuddled up in bed when Derek reaches beneath the pillow and pulls out the blindfold and cuffs. They're not gift wrapped, but it doesn't matter because they're so soft and silky and festive already. She's about to say thank you and wrap her arms around his neck when he grins sheepishly and says, "Shhhh…I'm afraid I'll change my mind."

So she lies back and closes her eyes. He fits the blindfold

over her eyes a little clumsily, his big fingers fumbling through her hair. She's tingling down to her toes in anticipation—it's all she can do to lie still and let him work. But she doesn't want to scare him, so she stays still, focuses on her breathing—in, out, relax—and enjoys the waves of excitement running through her body. When she opens her eyes, she can't see anything—a little aura of pink light through the fabric, but that's all.

He presses his lips to hers, and she realizes she's never kissed him before without watching him lean closer and closer in anticipation of the impending kiss. But now, she doesn't know what to expect, his lips are there and then they are elsewhere, and she doesn't know how to react, how to plan. Instead, his lips light unexpected little fires wherever they land, as though he's pressing fireflies to her skin. He is kissing the curve of her neck when he whispers, "Undress for me."

She feels a jolt of panic. Get undressed? How? She can't see anything. How will she know what she looks like? What if she does something stupid? But he is kissing her along the back of her ear, across the front of her shoulder blade, and she realizes it doesn't matter, that she'll do as he asks because she wants to, because he wants her to.

He helps her to stand, and then she hears him lie back down on the bed. The room around her feels too large, too empty, too alone, even though she knows it isn't. She fights the urge to reach out for something, anything—the dresser, the edge of the bed, the closet door—and instead reaches down to find the tie of her robe. She unties it slowly, then slides it off her shoulders and lets it fall to the ground. Then, she takes a deep breath, and pulls her tank top slowly over her head and throws it over her shoulder. Her nipples are erect from the excitement and the cold air makes them pucker even more. Then she leans down, drops her panties down over her feet, and stands back up.

She hears Derek sigh, and tries to imagine where he is in the room, what he's doing. Then his hands are on her, trailing down her hips and across her thighs, and she realizes he's sitting on the bed and she must be standing right in front of him. He takes her ass in his hands and pulls her toward him, them runs his tongue across her belly button, down her thighs.

"Lie down," he says, and it doesn't even sound like his voice. It's gruffer somehow, more forceful. "Put your arms up," he says, and she does, feeling his strength as he holds both her hands above her with one of his own. Then she feels him slide the cuffs around her wrists, their furry softness caressing her skin, and then tightening and pulling them just enough so that she can't slide out. He hooks them to something—she's not sure what—and suddenly she can't move.

"Okay?" he asks tenderly, and she can't do anything but nod. She's not sure what she feels—excitement, anticipation, fear, desire—she wants him to do whatever he wants to her. She would say yes to anything he asked.

She realizes there is silence all around her. She can't hear or feel Derek anywhere. Her skin comes alive, and she imagines this is what it's like to be in a horror movie, where you know something's coming for you, but you don't know what it is or where it's going to come from. Or like being prey—every nerve, every muscle twitching, ready to react with a flight or fight response. "Derek?" she whispers. She's afraid to break the silence, but she feels like she has to do something. "Derek?"

She doesn't hear anything. A pull on the cuffs only seems to draw them tighter around her wrists. Is he sitting there watching her? Did he leave her here? What if he's taping her? She knows, of course, that he would never do any of these things, but the longer she waits the more the fear creeps in.

Then, finally, she hears a noise. She pricks her ears in that direction, feeling like a wild animal. Is that him? Is it the cat?

She can't tell. Her senses are deceiving her. Something cold brushes against her stomach, and she has a moment of near panic—she's ready to rip the cuffs right off—but then she feels Derek's tongue too, next to the coldness, and hears him crunching something in his teeth.

He runs his tongue, along with the ice, up her stomach, leaving a tingling trail of heat and cold, until he reaches her chest and the ice melts. Her stomach does somersaults as he winds his cool tongue around one nipple and presses his palm firmly between her legs. She presses against the flat of his hand, willing him to touch her, stroke her, enter her. She has forgotten she is handcuffed to the bed, that she cannot see. All of her senses are focused on just one spot—she feels that if he doesn't split her open soon she will explode.

"Please...," she whispers, "Please...."

"Please what?" Derek asks as he enters the bedroom. She didn't even hear him come in, and her face flushes with embarrassment. She thinks about pretending she was asleep, then thinks better of it and hands the catalog over to him.

"Please...please buy me these," she says softly, pointing to the silk bonds with one tired, trembling finger.

Buckle Fucker

Rakelle Valencia

I had been sucked down into the chute jerking my head up in desperation, searching for help, to find that she was all business. Her hands clawed my thick, protective vest with the same tenacity as the others. Hands that lifted me upright, back onto the bronc, and I had wished I could feel them on my skin. Her hands were strong, professional, serious, determined. I knew this in seconds as they gripped my thick, Kevlar vest. And I thought I knew what kind of woman she would be just by her hands.

Those long fingers had instantly intrigued me. The digits led to muscular yet feminine hands with veins pulsing in excitement. The pointer finger on her right was crooked with a thin, white scar marking flesh from nail to knuckle. A woman's working hands fascinated me so. I wanted to run my tongue along that scar, caress it, follow its trail, draw the marred appendage into my hungry mouth. And I had chastised myself because my brain was in the wrong game at that moment.

Shaking my Stetson-covered head, I tried to get back into

my ride, envisioning how the bucking horse would twist and writhe beneath me, this one first going to the left away from my hand then knowing to slam right when I began to overcompensate. Of course I wasn't planning to overcompensate. I had been planning to walk the edge and get her to buck out straight and strong, picking up points by stroking long, dotted lines with my spur rowels.

The mare was hot and fresh, not yet used hard at this level, which meant she was a wild card, not consistent. I'd ridden her before, and she was an honest bucker with a few tricks up her sleeve that would become known as her routine romp when she worked more.

The red mare tossed her tangled mane in angst then lathered into a captured frenzy, banging the steel panels, making me need support once again to keep from falling underneath those large hooves. A cowboy down in the chute is dead, or at least hurtin' enough not to be makin' any rides at that rodeo. I stabbed my toes on the rails and wiggled behind a bit, out of the sweet spot, until the horse settled. Hands were all over me still, keeping me safe, voices urging me on.

Our eyes met. The rugged, lady cowboy on the chute crew had greenish-brown eyes that just about melted my watery blues, and I had hoped she knew that I was thanking her for her help, for her hands. She smiled with only half of her face, a cockeyed grin. I was careful not to nod as that would throw the gate open.

I'd been riding horses since I was a kid and only recently had I given myself over to trying the bred broncs, bred for bucking. I'm not too sure that the whole idea sits well with what I like. I mean, where I come from, we ride horses to gentle 'em, to get 'em good and broke. But hell, this rodeo deal gets me laid.

Unfortunately, I was thinkin' on that and not on the ride under me as I scooted into my rigging, pressing the smooth, tight, bulging crotch of my Wrangler jeans against my hand, wiggling into the sweet spot once again. I stretched out good, having contact, spurs to silky shoulders, for when I came out of the chute. I nodded, tucked my chin and threw my upper body back, lining out from the point of shoulders with both rowels.

I remember that it was a terrific start, very classic for a hop or two. I remember that I had forgotten who I was on, searching my head for a name when my brain went elsewhere, remembering that I hadn't caught the woman's name, the chute crew, lady cowboy's. But I shouldn't have been thinking about her.

I got too lost in daydreaming like a moon-eyed schoolboy over that cowgirl, and couldn't come up with any thoughts on this particular horse's routine. I'd had it at the forefront of my mind once. Now there was nothing. Right when I needed to know this horse the most...

Well, that red, bucking mare switched on me. I promptly caught air between my denim-clad ass and the red, hairy carnival ride, and I knew immediately what that meant. When the stadium audience viewed sunlight betwixt me and a bronc, I'd be gettin' off fast. Sure enough, that bucking mare asked me to leave, hard.

I didn't make the buzzer. In fact, I had barely made four and a half seconds. It wasn't the hang time that hurt, it was the landing. There wasn't going to be any trophy buckle for anyone to polish off of me tonight. Might as well collect my rigging and head out.

Climbing the chutes to exit the arena, I was thinking on how much I would be missing that weight strapped to the front of my midsection, moving with me, yet causing just enough friction for me not to forget it was there, all the while trying to remember the damn name of that red mare.

"Maria," she said, that chute crew, lady cowboy breaking into my thoughts.

"Nope. Wasn't anything as pretty as that. More like Buckle Fucker," I replied in a frump, dragging my rigging over the stock rails, landing on the pleasure side of the fence, the business aspect left behind in four and a half seconds.

"Well that's a new one. I don't believe I've ever been called that before. At least not to my face." She shuffled and pretended to huff with that slanted grin. "The mare's name was Two Steppin'. Do you dance?"

My gritted, stubbed fingernails picked at the tape securing the rosin-pasted glove. "Only in the arena with a four-legged partner." What I should have said was "yah, sure, any time, anywhere," but I was pretty soured with myself, not to mention embarrassed at that point.

Watching my struggle in unraveling the tape, she reached to unzip the shock-absorbing armor engulfing my torso and ran her hands over my chest, one down my stomach and past my belt, ever-so-slowly. Stiff batwing chaps hit the cement aisle of the grandstands, tottering on their own to remain erect, before giving up and collapsing in an expensive heap of multicolored hide. My glove dropped to join them as this Maria twisted her long, thin, strong fingers into the front of my striped Cinch shirt, popping several of the pearly snaps.

When her lips touched mine I was still dazed. My hands went to either side of her waist feeling the thick, tooled leather that I trailed with clammy digits to an engraved hubcap the size to fit a sports car. I jerked the silver plate like opening a can of tonic. Instead of the fizz I heard the roar of the crowd, reminding me that we were center-stage of the stands.

I felt my ears get hot, knowing that my face must have reddened brighter than that flaming mare I had just come off of. Lust welled within my head and grew within my Wranglers but I hitched her buckle back up and bent to grab my gear.

"Where ya going, cowboy?" she asked.

"Back to the hotel, ma'am." I tipped my hat in the most gentlemanly manner.

"Can I come?"

A grin ripped my face apart to a crease greater than a river gorge through the Grand Canyon. "As many times as you want," I replied and chauffeured her to my dented pickup truck, making doubly-sure that the door had latched properly closed.

She was forward. I liked that. And she was no road whore. I'd seen some that were battle weary—you know, rode hard and put away wet. I stayed clear of those.

I'd seen Maria around many of the rodeos. She came from good, hard-working class, blue collar. My guess would have been that daddy was a stock contractor. How else would a lady have been working behind the chutes?

In my room, I dropped my gear and popped her buckle again, sliding the leather from its keeper. She stared me in the eyes, capturing my stubbled jaw in her palms to drag me in for a kiss. My tongue was trying to probe hers when she shoved my shoulders downward with insistence, directing me to my knees.

The hubcap was real. This lady was a team roper from what I could read of the engraving blurred in my vision, being too close to the end of my nose. She was a header I guessed. Maria unsnapped the fancy silver plate the rest of the way and peeled it from the leather strap, dropping it with a clink upon my rigging. Her slender fingers entangled snakelike into my short, brown hair, knocking my Stetson to the worn rug, shoving my face to the copper-colored button of her jeans.

The smell of wash-detergent and horses and leather and musk appealed to my nostrils as if baiting me in. I reached for the riveted button with a jerk of both hands and had the gritty, little zipper down before she clasped my wrists and hog-tied them by the leather strap of her belt. When I looked,

I knew my eyes had begged of her. She wavered, releasing her hold, the two of us peeling her slim-fit Wranglers to stack higher on her boot tops.

I felt her fingers in my hair again, smashing my face to her shaved, trimmed pubic strip. Maria jutted her pelvis forward, opening her lower lips along with her long legs, flattening my nose into her silky flesh. My tongue stabbed out at her, rewarded by a squeak then a low, rumbling groan. I lapped at her slit like it was an ice cream cone on a hot, muggy July day, clawing between her legs with my wrists still bound at her full asscheeks.

She started riding me as if she were at a jog on a hot-blooded quarter horse. My face was the seat of her saddle, my hair was the mane of her gelding or the horn of the pommel she held on to. And I could so go with that scenario because what I really wanted were those clenching thighs hugging my ears to finish the scene.

I tugged at her captured boots, jeans wringing the leather uppers to create manacles that I fought against in her behalf. My insistence and the awkwardness of my trapped wrists tripped her, throwing us both off balance, Maria landing without injury upon the late '60s, early '70s avocado-colored bed covering.

It was fortunate that my recent meager rodeo winnings did not allow for a large suite. The rundown hotel sported rooms no bigger than a box stall, the bed, with its well-bleached, well-starched sheets, demanding most of this space. All of this made it easier to remain on my knees, no floor length to cover as I crouched by the side of the bed throwing long, naked, white, smooth legs over my shoulders.

I love the smell of women. I love the taste of them, the feel of them. I love to please them, especially when I can hear their whispered thanks, their moans and groans of appreciation, their grunts of gratitude. I love women, all types, shapes, sizes.

All women. The mere sounds of Maria panting and squirming in delight made me reach for my swollen crotch. Dust-covered, sweaty jeans stood sentinel against calloused palms, resisting my haste to stroke myself to a quick, spewing cum. I struggled, ripping and pulling at pants and jockstrap to spring my throbbing hard-on.

Once loosed, I humped at the quilt hanging from the side of the bed, grinding against the firm mattress and the seam where it met the box spring. I needed something more than my own dry, bound hands, but my body was stuck in place, my mouth refused to give up its territory on a whim.

As my prick jumped on its own accord, I thrust two fingers into Maria, and her hole gave in warm wetness, dribbling creamy slickness down her crack toward a puckered, darkened anus which kissed at wandering fingertips as delicately and deliberately as she had kissed my lips at the rodeo.

Maria shrieked in spasms and sat bolt upright, yanking me from between her moistened legs by my ears. Her hands shredded through my striped Cinch shirt; the snapping, almost cracking of those little pearly white closures rang like firecrackers, and satiny legs fell free from my shoulders.

Gooseflesh rose over my chest with the caress of her strong hands. My body was unaccustomed to the touch of a forward woman, a muscle-laden, ranch-hardened, determined woman. Maria's hands took what they wanted, much like the woman herself. And I had known, somehow, that she would be like that. But that was no solace for my aching, rigid prick.

She tweaked at my nipples, nearly sending me flat to the floor, and sucked my mouth earnestly. Maria wrapped firm fingers around my engorged dick and plied me with strokes of friction, skin moving alive and hot in her palm over and separate from the blood-filled tissues inside.

My body collapsed away from her touch, my cheek slapping the flesh of her lap, my lungs gasping for air, stomach concave, jerking my erection from her grip. It was too much, way too much. Her powerful hands dominated my entire being and I would have to waive control to take the ride.

Maria clasped both sides of my head like a vise and licked her tongue about my lips as she rocked backward, flat to the bed, dragging me with her. Legs engulfed me. Knees hooked onto my hips. Ankles crossed over my back. My elbows at her ears. With one massive hug, Maria had my cock lined up and driven into her.

Wind whistled through her pouty, swollen, sensuous mouth as if she had just dipped into the water of a soaking, soothing bath. I ground my teeth and grunted much as I had when I hit the arena dirt with a dull thud of pain and frustration. I couldn't do this, although I told myself that I could in my head. I mean, I could, but the whole thing was going to be over quick. I probably wouldn't even make four and a half seconds.

I was barely holding on, thinking of anything else that I could to make this ride last when my ass rang out with the slap of her hand. I pulled back in reaction, putting air between me and the saddle. I knew it was over. Time to get off.

One of Maria's hands clawed into the back of my neck, the other smacked my tense, undulating buttocks again, and again.

My throat growled until it was raw with fire, my body pumped uncontrollably with wave after wave of jism unloading into her, into Maria. It wasn't my dick that came, it was my entire rugged, worn body pounding and riding to a motion not of my making.

I knew my asscheeks were reddened. I could feel the warmth of their glow. No matter how many years they had been hardened in the saddle I knew that there was always that ride that would sore them up. For me, that ride was Maria.

Noticing too late that her hands had both descended to my

hips as her legs fell open, the toughened cowgirl marked me with fingernails to my shoulders as if spurs were rolling over a bucking horse. At the same time, her pussy clamped on to my softening prick threatening with contracting strength to cut it off. I drove into her. Maria let out a cry that made sweat trickle the rain gutter between my shoulder blades and she writhed and twisted in carnal pleasure beneath me.

In the morning she was gone. I rolled out of bed to unceremoniously fall in a heap on the threadbare rug, rubbing first one chafed wrist then the other, surprised by the feeling of being rode hard and put away wet. Shaking my head into focus, my vision was teased by the shiny, hubcap-sized buckle holding down a little note torn from the bedside hotel pad: GOOD RIDE. YOU EARNED IT. Grabbing the buckle I read the engraving: CHAMPION HEADER.

It Ain't Always Easy

Tom Piccirilli

This is where things get a little funky.

She reaches into the nightstand drawer and finds the handcuffs. You know what's coming but it's already in motion, and despite the sharp prodding under your heart you realize you've got to ride it out.

So, okay—

She lets loose with a low gurgling noise that's supposed to make her sound like a shocked Sunday school teacher. Actually it sounds like something LeeLee the computer-literate gorilla at the San Diego Zoo makes when she's in a hot mood and typing out FUCKME FUCKME FUCKME on her little palm pad while chasing the handlers around her cage.

LeeLee's a monkey of strong wants. She's been on the news every night this week, with zoo officials promising to fly in a mate for her from the central highlands of Zaire. The nervous handlers look violated and in need of extensive therapy.

The window's open just enough that the car alarms, shouts, sirens, and other midsummer street noise draw your attention. The breeze circles the room and pats the nape of your neck like the soft hand of your last lover.

Actually, she never patted you there and didn't love you and didn't have soft hands, but you compensate with a vivid imagination and maudlin sentimentality.

This one, her name's Kathleen. You know her from the neighborhood and you've scoped each other in the bar scene before, but tonight something clicked. The right amount of liquor, the lack of choice in the crowd.

So—she's got the handcuffs and she's twirling them around on the chain, eyebrows arched like she's expecting you to explain yourself.

Like you'll say, Hey, I'm into the bondage scene, baby!

Like you'll say, Those old things? I've got a pair of fur-lined restraints in the closet!

Like you'll say anything except, Those cuffs, they were my father's. He was a cop. He died on the job. Heart attack, not like he was shot trying to stop a bank robbery. I keep them around for reasons I don't comprehend. I didn't much like the man, and he probably thought less of me. His badge is in there too. It's not gold, he never made detective.

You keep a tight lip and try to grin at her. It doesn't really work. Your charm is lacking more and more these days.

Instead, she's waiting and losing patience. You stare at each other for a few more seconds. As if it was all rehearsed many times before and you've missed your cue, she makes the horny gorilla noise again.

You might have your hang-ups but you need some affection too, and the craving is on you in a rush and you reach for her. This one, she moves aside and gives you a wide leering smile. You jumped too fast and now she knows she's in charge. It never comes down to who's strongest, but who's weakest.

She tells you to roll over on your back.

You can either buck the situation or go with it. You've

gone with so little over the years that abruptly you feel like doing something you've been told to do.

Fine. You roll onto your back and you see that she doesn't really know what she's doing either. She frowns like she's trying to figure things out step by step, and tells you to take your clothes off.

So now you've gotta get up, get naked, and then get back on the bed and roll over on your back. When you're a square wedge of vanilla, this shit ain't as easy as it looks on the videos.

Kathleen, she puts one cuff on your right wrist and then notices that you don't have a wrought-iron headboard she can just stick the chain through. Either she closes the other cuff on your left wrist, which really isn't doing too much in the foreplay department, or she has to improvise.

You've got to give it to her, she's making a valiant effort. She tells you to get off the bed and lie on the floor.

Whatever. You sit on the throw rug and she orders you to scoot.

Scoot? Which way?

This way, she says, so you scoot this way.

Further, she says, and there's an odd tremble of frustration in her voice, as she realizes this takes a little practice. Time to figure out how to use these props, play the game right. You scoot more and more, getting rug burns on your ass. Some folks would think that adds to the ambience, but it just stings.

Scoot!

I am!

More!

Jesus Christ, lady, the fuck you want me?

There, she says, and you get the picture. You slide down to the radiator and she snaps the other cuff in place.

It looks more fun when they do it on the nasty-sex cable channels. There, everybody is greasy and laughing and raring to go. Here, it feels like you've been kidnapped by the Sandinista rebels.

Kathleen does a slow striptease act, humming to herself like she's on stage, but slightly embarrassed by her own grin. You know the feeling. You're both acting roles that weren't exactly designed for you, but what else is there to do in the city on a Sunday night at 3:00 a.m. except give it a whirl?

She's pretty good actually, taking her time and moving around the room with authority, giving you a peek here and there. Flashing the undersides of her tits, the hint of an inner thigh. You like what you see. You're aroused and sort of surprised about it. You'd think the harsh pressure of the radiator vents digging into your back might be too annoying, but now it's pretty much all right. So long as nobody puts the heat on.

You're supposed to be the submissive here, the one who takes orders. The pawn, the tool, the toy who waits, but to hell with all that.

You start giving her the mastering gaze. It usually doesn't work. You try to influence your will upon the world like everyone else. This one, she sidles closer doing a baby-girl pout, and drops her clothes with an air of virginal please-don't-hurt-me.

You'd think that being shackled to ninety-year-old piping might be a giveaway to helplessness, but it's not. You arch your hips a little, pressing your cock forward. She squats above and eases onto your shaft.

She's still giving you the baby bottom lip but instead of thrusting up into her for all you're worth, you slip your free hand to the side of her face, move to nuzzle her neck. She sinks another inch into your lap. You both grunt but there's almost something sweet about it now. This bondage thing, it's for the pros. You try this shit without reading a study guide or two and you might hurt yourself.

Except for the naked woman slamming on your groin,

you're in somewhat the same position as everybody your father ever arrested. You try to hold her in place but you've only got the one hand to do it with. She grunts deep in her chest, and it's a noise that tickles your nuts.

There's an animal inside all these modern sensitive-man neuroses that keep your analyst's kids in college while you try to figure out why you feel guilty for a normal mortal's sins.

The atmosphere shifts some as she lets out a laugh. You can't help yourself and you do the same. It feels good, sort of. Kathleen's bouncing around faster and faster, and you're digging the feeling but it's still rough going. You're just doing your best not to pop your shoulder out of the socket. Every time she zigs left you've got to zig with her or you'll tear your rotator cuff. It happened once during college football and probably cost you a very minor career.

It's hard to shake off the absurdity of yourself in the moment, but when she grinds into you like this, leaning over to whisper in your ear, you can nearly let go. It's nice enough. She's got the rhythm down just right and her voice is sufficiently sweet to make you think this might not be just a one-night stand.

That's gotten more important as you've grown older, though maybe it shouldn't have. You suck on her nipples and thrust into her, moaning in a whiny way that doesn't befit a man. She doesn't seem to mind, and that's all it takes to bring you to the edge.

But you've got your duties, so you hold off and wait until she's shuddering, leaning forward to perch herself against the wall. She slips and clonks the radiator and the vibration races through the cuff and rattles your teeth.

She's banging away like crazy and you're really hoping she's getting off because you're patient, but you can't sit on this fence forever. She screams, Now, which may or may not be a order.

It doesn't matter much. She's hit the spot and you fire off like you're getting paid for it.

You both take a couple minutes to wind down, catch your breath. Now that it's over, you can see she's a little worried. Your wrist is bleeding and your elbow's scraped and bruised. There's a price to pay for every damn thing you do.

Where's the key? Kathleen asks.

You blink a few times to get the sweat out of your eyes.

Hey, you tell her, that there, that's a good question.

You think it might be in the nightstand.

She rummages around and says she can't find it.

You have visions of the landlord coming in with the plumber discovering you here like this, the guy screaming about how the radiator is dented. How it's going to come out of your deposit. The plumber just standing there and laughing, saying it's the third time this month he's found some schmuck cuffed to the piping.

Wait, wait, she goes, here it is, I've got it.

She lets you loose and leads you to the bathroom and swabs your cuts with witch hazel and gives you two aspirin. Even she knows you're going to hurt in the morning. She washes up beside you and dresses carefully.

Before she applies a new coat of lipstick she hugs you to her and plants one on your mouth. The moment lengthens and becomes more tender, and then she's out of your arms.

She's pulled out a pad and pen from the drawer and written her phone number on it. Her full name beneath. No smiley faces or happy hearts with wings. Nothing cutie-pie about it, you're already past that. Which is encouraging, all things considered.

Kathleen draws the back of her hand across a sheen of salt on your chest and then she's out the door.

Dad. Dad, maybe he's looking down going, Son, the police force has rules about this sort of thing. Those handcuffs, they aren't a toy.

You head to the kitchen and grab an ice pack for your shoulder. You get back on the bed and hit the remote. LeeLee's trainers are looking even worse for wear, their eyes wide, their terror pretty damn obvious. In the background, LeeLee is typing out commands and glowering at the camera.

It reminds you that you haven't been to the zoo in a long time. You reach for the phone and groan in pain.

Jesus, how do they do it, the pros? Hanging upside down with chains threaded through their pierced nipples, leather plugs jammed all over the place. What, they go to classes for this, use safety lines? They've got trainers? Stunt coordinators?

You give Kathleen a call. She's not home yet but you leave a message, asking if she wants to go to the zoo on her day off. A regular kind of date, with ice cream and balloons and stuff.

It might scare her. It might piss her off. You've run into those types before, the ones who want to screw but don't want to go catch a movie. Maybe you're even one of them, but you just can't be sure.

So now you look back to the television and LeeLee's got some poor bastard cornered in her cage. She's typing furiously at the weeping keeper, and you try to imagine what kind of love letters she might be composing.

You grab the pad and start writing your own, hoping you can compare.

See Dick Deconstruct

Ian Philips

I'm thinking of an image. It's from one of those stories where Our Father throws Lucifer out of the house for good. I can't remember which.

Maybe *Faust.*

Maybe *Paradise Lost.* It doesn't matter. All I remember really is the image.

It's of the future Satan sitting among us and forever looking back toward the one place to which he would never be able to return. And this, of course, leads to more stories. Ones where, to soften the pain of remembrance, The Fallen One tries to stick it to The Man by sticking it to one of The Man's favorites.

Think Job. Think Jesus.

In a way, this is one of those stories.

Sort of.

I have no idea what The Man or any other god thinks about my little boy. But I do know that before we met he was fast becoming a darling of the Academe. Not any just any old university. The Academe—site of all discourse and inquiry located in that great metanarrative in the sky.

I'd seen his name several times before he told it to me that night. He'd been a contributor to various anthologies. Ones with glossy covers in garish colors drawn on a computer. Covers that promise a mondo-pomo-homo-a-go-go world within. Then you turn the page. Instead it is only a book filled with straggling bands of menacing, jibbering words from the clans Tion or Ize. Words that must wander those pages forever at war—sometimes even with their own in the same sentence. Leaving behind a field of white, strewn with participles dangling, dying.

To be honest, I don't know if it was just dumb luck or synchronicity that led me to answer his personal. And, after what I did to him our first night, he's the one who'll want to dig up Jung and ask him whom or what to thank. I merely made the most of a moment.

His personal? Something about a Queer, White Dork, this weight and that height, goatee and glasses. Has a hard spot for hairy, horny daddies. Grooves on the transgressive in theory and praxis. Then the standard blah, blah, blah.

I had no plans for what we'd do if things clicked. Not even after I recognized QWD's name. My inspiration came only after he offered me a cigarette.

I smiled and shook my head. His brand, not his offer, had surprised me. American Spirit. This boy had spent a lot of his time and someone's money redecorating his mind in early '70s French cultural critique. I'd expected Gitanes. Or maybe, in the down-and-dirty spirit of Genet, that he'd have rolled his own. But no, he smoked American Spirit—filtered. He'd been out here on our brittle bit of the Rim of Fire longer than I'd thought.

He lit up. A real feat since we were sitting outside this café on Market Street. That shouldn't mean anything to you unless you've been to San Francisco in the summer. It was late afternoon when we put our first pints on the table. And a late summer afternoon in San Francisco means that the fog flying in over Twin Peaks uses Market Street as its landing strip.

So as gust after gust touched down, he lit up. On the third try. And, by then, he was curled so tightly around the cigarette he looked like a fetus hugging its heart.

He sucked a few times on the burning paper and then spoke. I had the masculine signifiers he wanted—bulk, a beard—or so he said. But, he added, I was smaller than the men he'd been with before. And I thought, *Yes, I am small; beware the small.*

I know. I know. You probably don't give a shit what we said or what I look like. You only want me to describe my dick and what it did. I won't. Call me a tease, but we both know one man's dick is another man's dink is another man's dong. Besides, I'd rather give your puny little imagination a workout. So maybe I have one. Maybe I don't.

The boy and I kept talking. Through several more beers, cigarettes, a course of spring rolls and pad Thai, then along the streets and up the stairs to my apartment and down the hall to my bedroom.

We stopped beside my bed. I put one of my short, thick fingers to his lips. I stepped back. "Strip."

He nearly beamed. Quickly, he gripped the bottom of his terry cloth shirt of many colors and yanked it over his head and down his arms. His nipples stood out on the pale skin. Two dark dots. Alternating patches of muscle and bone. All strung together by a few hairs running from his breastbone to the rim of his shorts. He knelt and unlaced his Airwalks. They'd been the color of wet sand, but in the unsteady light of the room's candles I could barely see the whites of their laces or his socks. He put them all against the wall and returned to the spot beside my bed. He unbuttoned his shorts, let them drop, stepped out of one leg and, with his foot in the other, kicked them over toward his shoes. I could forgive this smiling eagerness to please as a bit of nervous excess, but that kick smacked to me of precociousness. My suspicion was confirmed when he tried to lock eyes with me as he tugged his white cotton briefs down over his budding cock and then his thighs. He had to look down once he got to his knees. As soon as his underwear was at his ankles, he raised his back so I could get a good view of his dick. It was long and fat like an animal's snout. It flopped against his balls while he shook one, then another, foot free.

It'll do, I thought.

I looked up and met his eyes. "It's interesting how it's often the choices made with the least thought that carry the most damning consequences." He blinked. "Like your high kick. Very precious. I don't like precious." His eyes widened. "Maybe I should just send you home...." He blurted out something. The beginning of a plea. I jerked my right index finger to my lips. He swallowed a paragraph of yet-to-be-spoken words.

"What—no one's ever spoken to you in the conditional? I said 'maybe.' I said 'should.' You'll stay as long as I want you to stay. And that might even be the whole night if—if you obey my one rule: you may speak; but each sentence may have only three words; and each word may have only one syllable. Otherwise, you can jabber away at the cab driver on your way home. Agreed?" He nodded. "Are you sure you don't need me to diaper that mouth with a gag?" He shook his head so hard his balls swung from thigh to thigh.

Always the student, I thought, *craving tests. Good, we'll begin with the hardest one first.* So, I decided to take a few long minutes and bind him tight with the one thing I knew he feared most—silence.

It began when my face stiffened into a stare. He smiled nervously for the first few seconds. I think it was a minute before I even blinked. By then, his lips had filled in the gash of teeth. We listened to our breathing. To the sputtering of the candles.

Finally, I turned and walked out of the room. I left him alone in the squirming shadows. It would be three, maybe five minutes more before I'd return with a wad of pink fabric tucked in my right fist.

I tossed it toward his feet. The wad fluttered up into the air and blossomed into a pair of pink silk panties, a size 5 women's, a snug fit even with his narrow hips. The one-petaled flower fell fast to the ground. "Put them on."

He crouched to pick them up. He fumbled trying to get the crotch going the right direction. He stepped out of one leg and turned the material around the pole of his other. The panties slipped up his calves and over his knees. Then, he had to tug slowly up along his slim thighs, over the ass I'd yet to see, and around his resistant cock. The waistband snapped at his hips and the dick was plastered against the right side of his pelvis. He looked up. Either the material chafed or he was pantomiming defiance. I didn't care.

"Take off your glasses."

He nearly chirped. Something about no longer being able to see.

"What's to see?"

I walked up to him, pulling a strip of leather out of my back pocket. I let it hang out of my right hand, though I doubt he could see this. I got behind him and lifted it above my head, then over his. I tied it around his eyes. I stepped back in front of him. As I pressed my hands close to his eyes to adjust the blindfold, I could smell his face. It was bitter with smoke and fear. I lingered long enough for his cold skin to feel the warmth from my breath.

I moved away. "You've talked a lot tonight. Most of it, I enjoyed. In fact, by dinner, I felt like I was back in school. Shooting the shit at three in the morning with a paper due at ten." I paused to cross the room and return with my butterfly knife.

"I just have one question. It's about what makes a man. You seem to know. Well, you did in that article for *Homosex(e)*." He started as he realized how naked he'd become. "What was your thesis for that one? Something about 'penetration being a mode of production in the manufacturing of the masculine.'" I stopped to let his own stilted words limp over to him.

"I'm sorry. Here I am contextualizing my question and I haven't even asked it. Let me try this again. First, I'll introduce some givens, then the question." I opened my left hand. "This is a dick," I said while I pushed my palm flat against the pink panties and then his prick until each were mashed against the wall of pelvic bone. I waited for his dick to stiffen and push back. Hand and cock then began a little dance until the hand had shuffled the tip of the dickhead up and under the strangling elastic waistband. Below it, a swelling pink stem was pointing toward the ceiling.

"Then," I said as I plucked the head, nearly in full purple bloom, "to use your own terms," and I pulled flower, stalk, and the taut rim of the panty out to me as far as I could—I almost lifted him up off his feet—"there's what you called the concretized phallus." And now my right hand and its knife reached into the gap between his dick and his belly.

I turned the knife on its side and stroked the dull edge of the cold blade up the shaft, prickling with hairs and goose bumps. "Actually, anything with a point'll do." My left hand slowly let go so that only the knife held his cock and the over-extended waistband in place. "So here's my question. If I took this," and I flicked my left index finger at his dickhead, as if it were a marble and this were a game. I paused to feel it thud against the warming metal. "If I took this and left you with this," I pushed the concretized phallus against the cock that was trapped on the other side by my finger, "would you still be a man?"

I waited.

The muscles of his stomach flinched, shaking the skin that rippled the air that stirred the hairs on my arm that held the knife. I hoped that this was his answer. I waited. It was.

I almost smiled. I was beginning to enjoy our date. For now I could spend the rest of it teaching him the deeper meaning of his wordless response.

I pulled the knife out in one stroke. The panties snapped his prick back in place. He gasped. He was stung but uncut. I grabbed both his hands and pulled them toward me and the bed as I jumped up onto it. I rolled off the other side still holding him. I let go and he lay facedown across it. I took his left hand and tied it to the left post of the black metal headboard. I moved around the bed knotting and cinching his three remaining limbs to the three remaining corners. Then I stood. Breathing deeply. I'd worked fast and was winded. I'm sure he could hear my snorts over the thudding of his own heart.

For the first time, I saw his pink ass. I jerked the waistband down and under the curves of his butt. The smooth, round, white cheeks plumped like breasts lifted by an underwire bra. I cupped them with both my palms. They grew warm. *Pap. Pap. Pap.* Three swift slaps to warm them more. I allowed a few moments of silence. Enough time for his ears to stop ringing. So he'd be able to hear this. I yanked the tail of my leather belt out of its buckle so hard that it creaked. Next belt and buckle slithered into my hand. The treated and tanned skin groaned as I bent it, then snapped it taut.

"You cocky little fucker. Answer me." The dead animal's hide slapped across the hide of my little live one. The echo of the clack somersaulted around the room. The candles wavered. But he said nothing. This boy who, in print, had never made his point in under 15,000 words said nothing. I was growing quite excited as I realized there might be a spark of brilliance in him after all.

"Or maybe you can't." I began to punctuate each sentence with the end of my belt. "Not because you're too dumb." *Thwack.* "Not because you're too smart." *Thwack.* "But because you're one of those pitiable scholars who can't speak without citing someone else." *Thwack.* "Must explicate." *Thwack.* "Must legitimate." *Thwack.* "Must use the *f*-word." *Thwack.* "Foucault." *Thwack.* "Foucault, Foucault, Foucault." *Thwack, thwack, thwack.*

His ass was pink again. Almost roseate. I took my left hand and let my fingers survey those patches that even in this dim dark shone. "Such a hot ass," I said. I lowered my head toward it. My tongue slipped and slid over the nearly hairless skin as if it were ice. Ice that seemed cold and smooth, but my tongue grew warm against it, felt its throb. "Such a hot ass," I said again and left the room.

The kitchen isn't far from the bedroom. A few feet. He must have heard me open the mouth of the freezer. Heard it sing its one long, cold note. Heard the spine of the ice tray crack in my hands. "Miss me?" I think he moaned some answer. "Miss this?" I dragged my tongue back along the trail left by my belt. I'm certain he was groaning when I took my tongue and pried at his crack, digging deepest near his hole. He tried to push his ass closer to my face. So trusting for one I'd thought so critical.

I lifted my head. Now, before my saliva could dry, I pressed down the melting cube. His butt muscles clenched. I retraced where the tongue, first of my belt and then of myself, had been. His whole body tensed as I pushed the cube down between his cheeks. "Such a hot ass," I whispered. I nudged the ice over his hole. It was sweating its own lube. I took my thumb and ground it into his asshole. He rolled his head over the pillow, biting at it. "Go ahead. You still have your dick. Be a man and scream." He tried to kick me off. Maybe he yelped. I dug at the decomposing ice cube with my fingernail. It plopped out. I slid it down toward his balls, leaving it to melt.

He began to twist against his ropes. All this show to shake off a shrinking chip of ice. I grabbed the scruff of his neck. Then I gave his butt a swift, sharp blow with the belt. He was still.

"You lied to me." I struck him again. "I've read everything you've been able to get published so far. You posited yourself over and over as a master theorist. Acted like you could demystify any obfuscation thrown your way. Like you were going to deconstruct the cosmos. Down." *Thwack*. "And down." *Thwack*. "And down." *Thwack*. "Until your praxis led to your dick. But why'd you stop there, boy?" *Thwack*. "What's so fucking special about your dick?" *Thwack*. "Is it magical?" *Thwack*. "Is that where you keep your male essence?" *Thwack*. "Your fucking trans-historical male essence." *Thwack*.

My left hand pulled at his hair and shook his head while my right hand flung the belt over my back. "You fucking hypocrite." *Thwack*. "You're nothing but a fucking," *thwack*, "closeted," *thwack*, "gender essentialist." Midstroke I stopped.

The harder I had hit, the higher his ass had leapt. On the last stroke, it jumped up to meet the belt. "No," I said out loud. I wasn't going to let him take control of the scene. This was about my revenge. Not his pleasure. Not tonight. Not on our first date.

I climbed onto the bed. I sat on his butt. Even through my jeans, I could feel the warmth of his skin. I sat there a moment, like a hen on her almost-hatched egg. I sat there a little longer. *Soon*, I thought with instinctual certainty, *soon*.

I leaned over his back until I was crouched over him, my belly pushing his head deeper into the pillow. I untied the left hand, then right. I crawled off him and the bed. I untied the left leg, then right. With both hands, I dug for the waistband that had now burrowed under the cheeks of his ass. I took the elastic and scraped it up along the skin. Before I let go, I gave a final yank and, *snap*, his panties were pulled up.

He began to mutter, reciting a rosary of "no's." He must have thought I'd untied him to send him home.

I tugged the ropes and the boy over to the chair and down across my legs until I felt the smooth fabric and the stiff cock slide across my right leg. I stopped when I had his dick bent over my knee just so. As if it had been scaling the outer wall of my leg and was now stuck, unable to heave the balls over.

Keeping the ropes in my left hand, I used my right hand to tear down his panties for the last time. I could feel the faint pulsing of his cock. It wouldn't be much longer before he wet himself. A few good slaps. So I decided to take my time. I ground my palm into the small of his back. Then I turned it on its side and started to push at that firm pink border wall. It gave a bit. A budge more. Then it recoiled, scooting my hand back to where it began.

Once more. This time I rolled my hand back onto its palm and let it curl into a fist. I plowed against the panty's waist. My knuckles, like the broad lip of a shovel, tried to lift it. Instead, they pushed under the rim and over the warm earth of his ass, until all momentum was lost and my hand flattened again, this time over that long fissure venting heat from its deep hole.

It was a pleasant moment. Unexpected. I dragged my hand out to try yet again. I placed my knuckles half on skin, half on silk. The boy squirmed a bit. I felt his cock flatten against my leg. He was growing impatient, insecure. Good. I would go even slower now.

I took my knuckles and rubbed at the edge of his right hip. Several tries and I got the rim to fold over on itself. I moved my hand toward the left hip. I did the same there. Soon I had the elastic turned in and out all along the edge of his butt. Now I would knead and roll and knead and roll the panties down as if I were making a pie crust. By the time I had them tightly under the ledge of his ass, I'd left his skin stinging, throbbing even, where the elastic, like a crude lawnmower, had torn out some of the few black hairs. And, though I was pleased, I could feel that my little man's interest had waned.

"Don't fall asleep on me, boy." I slapped his cold butt hard enough that my baby had to fill his lungs with air. "Do I bore you? Afraid you'll drift off before your queer elder passes the staff along to you?" I felt his body hesitate. He actually thought of answering me. "Oh, is that it?" I yanked the ropes and his wrists to the floor. I let my voice drift back in time and up an octave. "Fuck me, daddy, sir." Possessed, I began to bounce him against my knee and whack out a beat while I said, "Yes, sir. Yes, sir. Fill me full."

I stopped. His skin shook. His cock quivered. I leaned toward his left ear and whispered hoarsely, "I will, young man, but when I'm good and ready. Do I make myself clear?!"

I tugged the ropes again. His dick slid over my leg until his balls where flat against the side of it. "Huh?" I let go and he slunk back. I pulled again. "Well?" Then several more times until I knew these slow kisses between his silk and my denim must have been burning his dick. I could feel it swelling. I let him slide back and forth over my leg several more times as I kept shouting, "Do I?" The last time I didn't let go of the ropes. His cock and balls could barely teeter on the edge of my quite warm thigh.

"Now, you're going to tell me the truth. Aren't you, my queercore kid?" I slapped his ass twice. My palm stung. "You're going to tell me just how much of a lying essentialist hypocrite you are. Aren't you?" And I began to whack at the fleshy underbellies of his cheeks. Soft, fat, some muscle. I kept whacking all the while I kept shouting. "Aren't you a liar? Aren't you? Aren't you a fucking closeted essentialist? Queer theorist your ass. You never read Judith Butler. Did you? Did you? No, you hunched under your covers with a flashlight reading Judy Grahn and diddling yourself. Didn't you? Huh? Didn't you!"

By hitting the undersides of his buttcheeks, I'd been lifting his ass with each swat. Forcing him to rub his cock over and over against the hard muscle and bone in my leg. Making his own body first slap his balls and then mash them against the side of my thigh. So hard and so fast that the silk and denim were close to sparking. Even if I'd wanted to stop beating on his beet-red butt, it wouldn't have mattered now. He would've kept on humping my leg like the precocious panty-wearing dog he was.

Now, for every word I spoke, I batted at him with whatever strength was left in my nearly numb hand. "I know you read Mark Thompson's *Gay Spirit* over and over and over...." A "yes" spurt out of his mouth. "And over and over and over...." Another "yes." "Until you were weeping and clapping for faeries."

"YES!" He bucked forward and then rocked back on the fulcrum of my leg. It shook wildly, then he did. And did. And did. He was spewing a loud stream of "yes's" now.

I waited. He moaned, a low, hoarse sound, while rolling from side to side. I let go of the ropes and let my left hand stumble about until it found my knife again. I passed it over to my aching right hand. In a series of jerky, sawing strokes, I cut up the left side of his panties. When I reached the waist, they sprang apart. Now I leaned forward and cut open the right side. I put the knife down and steadied the boy's butt in my hand. With my left, I reached under his panting chest and pushed him up. Next, I grabbed the soaked front of his panties and pulled. My right hand felt the back end come slithering from both sides into his crack and up the crevice toward his balls. I watched his face contort as the fabric brushed up and up his still-too-tender shaft.

I gave a gentle shove to his left shoulder. He started slowly to drop down onto his knees, dragging his drooling dick along the denim, leaving behind a silvery streak like a snail's.

Once he landed on his knees, the real dumb show began. Bobbing up and down like a puppet with a broken string. One awkward attempt after the other to balance the weight of his body on his calves without letting them actually touch his butt. For a minute, it was amusing. Certainly more arousing than his striptease. But he kept on squirming and I grew bored. I bent sideways and fumbled along the floor. I was looking for the other thing I'd brought back with me from the kitchen. My hand patted the rug until I saw it glint in the candlelight. It was one of those tiny spoons used for cracking the shell of a soft-boiled egg and scooping out its jiggling white insides.

I opened my left hand and dug around in the pink wad with the spoon. I slid it under a shimmering blob of come. "Open wide." I turned toward him. Even with the blindfold, I could sense his blank stare. "Your mouth, brainiac." He hesitated then dropped his jaw. "Here comes a little spoon for my little man. Filled with man essence. Your man essence. Eat up." I rested the spoon's cold underbelly on his lower lip. Instinct—and that even crueler master, desire—made him do the rest.

"That's it. Eat up all the sacred man essence. We wouldn't want your sex to grow up without a gender, would we? No, we want your sex to have a gender," I said as I wrapped my hand around his plump cock and squeezed. "A manly gender."

I scooped out an even larger dollop. And, while he sucked down that spoonful, I smiled to myself. I was nearly humming by the time I made him lick the still-sticky insides of his panties. And it wasn't because I knew my little man was ready to be fucked. It wasn't even because I knew, from that night on, I could have this little man as I long as I wanted him. It was simply because nothing soothes the forever broken like breaking another.

A Hook and a Twist

Saskia Walker

"There's something about being tied up with rope that brings out the sex kitten in me," Lizzie commented, loudly, while spooning an impressive helping of creamy torte into her glossy, red moue.

Georgina folded her napkin, dabbed her mouth, and looked at her watch. She was about to leave, I could tell. Now don't get me wrong; Georgina isn't a prude, far from it. None of the three of us are shy, retiring types and Georgina has well and truly earned her "London Ladette" label. She's a man-eater of mega proportions; she just can't stand Lizzie's attention-seeking attitude. The fact that several occupants of the exclusive Covent Garden café had turned toward us would be enough to try Georgina's patience.

"Of course it has to be hand-maderope, and it has to be done with *true style*," Lizzie gushed, "and...by *a proper master*." She wiped a splash of cream from her lip and smiled down her nose at us, as if pleased to note she had the attention of her pupils. That rankled a bit, I have to admit, but I bit back my pride and returned her smile. You have to play dumb with Lizzie or she won't spill.

Georgina stood up, pulling on her coat, and announced that she would be late for a meeting if she didn't run for the tube. Me? I was hooked. Hell, I can suffer Lizzie's condescending attitude to find out some juicy tidbit. I'm always willing to consider new ways to stimulate my inner sex kitten, and whilst I had enjoyed sexplay with cuffs, belts, and scarves, the mention of handmade rope fascinated me.

Regrettably, I have to inform you that Lizzie's gushing narrative didn't give me the lowdown on the rope, and no amount of direct questioning helped. Instead, she wanted to impress me about her new bloke. She failed; he sounded more like an upper-class twit than "a proper master." But my curiosity had been baited, and the image of bespoke rope had lodged itself in my mind. What was it like? Would it release my inner sex kitten to be bound in it? What would it be like, running it through my fingers, assessing its power to restrain?

I did some research and located several sources for the material. I also discovered to my amusement that you could have it dyed to match other items in your sex assemblage. I even got some samples, and found that I especially liked the feeling of the hemp; its natural resilience and strength felt very sexy in my hands. I was interested, yes, but at first I couldn't find a playmate to explore my new fascination with. I mentioned it to two lovers, one of whom thought I was joking; the other thought I was a few sandwiches short of a picnic. No, it wasn't until Carl Sanderson walked into my life, several months later, that I had the opportunity to pursue the fascination for real.

Carl Sanderson was a management consultant who had been hired by the powers that be where I worked. He was the hatchet man, the man who would resolve time management issues with certain of our staff. I should have known he'd be into power games. The man positively exuded power. He walked into our offices one Monday morning and announced in no uncertain terms that he'd reviewed the procedures and things were about to be "well and truly shaken up." Yeah, I was prepared to be shaken up, in more ways than one.

I slid my glasses down my nose and observed him taking charge. He was attractive, not in the classical, good-looking sort of a way. He was strong and presentable, yes, but it was more like he had an underlying aura of power. Was it that quality that appealed to me?

His expression had a constant weathered look. You know, he'd been around the block a few times and his frown looked as if it was welded on. Even when he broke into a disarming grin, the frown was still there, like a testament to his intensity. His eyes were piercing blue, his hair a no-nonsense cut. Beneath the sleeves of his Saville Row shirts, I could see that his muscles were large and strong. Oh yes, Carl was every bit the veneered brute.

He walked from desk to desk in our open-plan offices, delivering snappy orders and tearing a strip off anyone who hadn't been performing to schedule. I was lucky, I had a ringside seat but I wasn't due for any flack. As the CAD assistant, I responded to the needs of the departments that were actually having the scheduling problems. And boy, did I enjoy watching Carl flex his muscles in the workspace. It was midsummer and steamy hot in the city; you know, sex was always on my mind. When he finally paced my way, I sat back in my chair and swiveled to face him.

"Megan Brody, now you don't appear to be on my list." He paused in front of my desk. He had a lopsided smile, very suggestive. "Shame," he added.

I gave him my best come-on smile and crossed my legs high on the thigh. "I could easily cause some trouble, if that's what you're after," I offered, hopefully.

"I'm quite sure you could," he replied, eyeing my bare legs

where my wraparound skirt had fallen open when I moved. He winked as he sauntered off. We had connected. I couldn't be more pleased.

By lunchtime that first day, I was entertaining full-blown fantasies about him. By the Tuesday, I'd snagged him for after-work drinks. By Thursday, we went for a bite to eat and then he asked me back to his place.

Dinner was light, by necessity—the heat, and the distraction of bodies wanting a different kind of feeding. We hit a noodle bar, sat on stools in front of the steaming kitchens and drank bottles of iced Asahi in an attempt to keep cool. I quizzed him about his work. The noise level grew as the place filled. He increasingly leaned toward me to chat. The smell of his aftershave and the musk of his body raced through my senses, dancing alongside the smells of food cooking and exotic spices. Every sentence was laden with double entendre, each discussion about power interchange and snapping people out of their daily routine. But you don't want me to tell you about our conversation; you want me to get to the juicy part. You want to know about the rope and how I found out he was one to play with. Okay. So he invited me home and we abandoned our food.

The air moved through the tube stations like a sirocco, a welcome breeze all the same. We stepped out by his riverside apartment block and a breath of air from the water gave my mind a moment of tingling clarity. It was short lived. It was a humid night, and his high-rise location only seemed to magnetize the heady atmosphere of the city.

He flicked on light switches as he walked inside, revealing a sparse bachelor pad with low leather sofas and a coffee table made out of a sheet of Perspex standing on stacked shot glasses. Cute, I thought. He leaned down to the stereo and flicked it on. Music sprang out, feeding background beats to me from every corner. I dropped my bag on a chair and smiled at him, and then I stalked closer to him, my hands on my hips. His gaze roved over my little black dress, my heels, and my thin, angular frame. The atmosphere between us was high with sexual tension.

He paused rather deliberately, as if to make sure I was watching, before hitting another switch. *What was this about?* A series of spotlights flashed on one by one in the far corner of the room, throwing into stark relief a gym area complete with weights bench, free weights, workout bars ranging high up the wall and floor-to-ceiling mirrors. Imagine my surprise when the area was fully lit and I saw the giant skein of wine-colored rope in the corner, knotted to the wall-mounted bars and dangling to the floor. I glanced back at him and noticed he was watching me, subtly, waiting for my reactions.

Well, what do you know?

I strolled over, my stacked heels clacking on the polished floorboards. I felt very self-aware, but why wouldn't I? We'd done more than enough flirting to flag up reciprocal interest. I'd taken his invitation to come into his space, and now I discovered he might be the perfect person with whom to explore my curiosity about rope. Besides, his eyes were boring into my back; my entire skin was taut with tension. He'd put himself and his toys on offer. It was up to me push things on; I could sense that. I supposed that I could choose to ignore the presence of the rope or I could give him a signal.

I didn't really have a choice, now did I? You know my curiosity had well and truly got the better of me. I stroked the rope with one tentative, curious hand. It wasn't hemp, like the samples I had enjoyed; it was synthetic, slicker, and somehow stronger. I glanced back at Carl. The hatchet man; all rippling muscle and contained sexual energy.

"Is it dyed to match anything in particular?"

His eyebrows lifted, but he was smiling. "Ah, I can tell you're a connoisseur."

I had to turn away so he wouldn't see me smile to myself. "Just curious," I replied, running it through my fingers. How many willing victims had he bound with it, I wondered?

"The weights bench," he replied, indicating the bench that stood alone beneath a spotlight.

The color did coordinate. Dark reds; like wine, like blood. I had a sudden image of a naked, pale body, spread-eagled over the vinyl bench, bound and trussed in the wine-colored rope, being fucked from behind. I glanced at him over the top of my glasses, and smiled.

He groaned. "I'm sure others have mentioned this, Megan, but the way you look over your glasses is such a turn-on."

Well, I know some men have a thing about girls in glasses, but his remark still surprised me. Was that why he had responded so readily to my flirting?

"In fact, it makes you look strong...powerful."

"Really?" I couldn't contain my surprise. Now there's a twist, I thought to myself. Is that what he wanted? For *me* to be the powerful one? I was thrilled! I love sexual role-play and power interchange. How could I not totally love the idea of dominating a brute of a man like Carl? Arousal sped through my veins. My inner sex kitten was up and out, skidding across the floor with claws out, ready to pounce. I was well and truly interested now.

I unlatched the skein of rope from the bars and began to unwind it as I walked back toward him. When I drew up in front of him, he grasped the rope and tugged. I held tight. The rope went taut between us. He had a wild look in his eye. For a moment I wondered if he had changed his mind. Did he want to take control, after all? I reached for his head with my free hand and pulled him down for an open-mouthed kiss. He moaned into my mouth when I slid my tongue along the inside of his lower lip, very deliberately, sensitizing him and beckoning his tongue into my mouth. I was loading up my arsenal of domina tricks. When I felt his hold on the rope slacken, I tugged. His body was against mine. Powerful, masculine: cocked and ready for action. I felt a surge of triumph. Oh yes, I was going to enjoy binding him up in his rope, gaining full control of his testosterone-fueled physique.

"I want to play, and I'd like you to strip," I murmured, as we pulled apart. I had said my thoughts aloud and almost jolted at the sound of my own voice. But my body was pulsing with arousal. I was on a roll. "I think we both know what's going on here, Carl, don't we?"

He nodded, his eyes bright with interest, his fingers quickly wending their way through his shirt buttons. He kicked off his shoes and abandoned his clothes.

"Sit here," I instructed. I patted the weights bench, while eyeing his body. My heart was racing, my focus closing in on bench, man, and rope.

His eyes never left mine.

I reached over and locked the back support into the upright position, so that his upper body would be on an incline. His cock was rising before my eyes, his body rippling with movement. He was flexing his corded muscles, preparing for what was ahead. I had to drag my gaze away as he took his seat and I moved to stand behind him.

Arms first. I braced myself for action and threw the rope out across the floor, shaking out the loops. Snatching up one end, I squatted down behind him, pulled his wrists together, and secured them inside a figure-eight knot. The rope coiled and twisted across the floor as I worked, alive and supple as a serpent.

He was watching me in the mirrors. "You're adept with knots," he commented and shook his head, disbelievingly, as if he'd made a real find. His expectations were now very high. My hands trembled slightly. I hoped I wasn't going to let him down! I silently ordered myself to go with the flow and follow my instincts.

"Blame the childhood holidays spent boating. My father was a fanatic."

"Oh, I'm not complaining."

I walked around him at that very moment and pulled the rope across his chest.

"Far from it," he added, as I began to truss him to the bench in true earnest.

His nipples were already hard. I wanted to see them trapped between two twists of rope. When I did exactly that, I thought he was going to raise the roof with his enthusiastic grunts.

"Fuck you're good," he muttered, his eyes going to the ceiling and husky laughter escaping from his lungs.

"Why, thank you." I was loving every moment of his submission.

The humidity levels only seemed to rise by the moment. I was creaming, my thighs slick with sweat, my G-string clinging to the damp heat in my groin.

I wound the rope around his torso and across his hips and thighs, carefully arranging it on either side of his cock, lifting his balls between the lines of rope to ensure a snug fit. He cursed under his breath, but I took a deep breath and didn't let it distract me from my purpose. When I had secured his ankles, tying him to the struts of the bench, I stood back to admire my handiwork.

What a sight!

His cock was dark with blood and distended to its limits, poking out demandingly between the ropes that contained him, the ropes that applied enough pressure to keep him on edge. His muscles seemed even stronger in their containment. His torso bowed under the rope, instinctively working against its enclosure. He was a gorgeous brute of a man, and I had him restrained.

Oh, it fast grew even hotter under those spotlights, fast grew even hotter when I stalked around him, admiring the sight from every angle, watching his growing anxiety with my hungry eyes. I stripped off my dress, my bra, and my G-string, kicking them across the floor. I kept on my stacked heels because they made me feel powerful enough to take him on, and the glasses, as a concession for Carl.

It was then that I caught sight of myself in the floor-to-ceiling mirror. For a moment, I was shocked. The chic designer frames perched on my nose were the only nod to socialization. I looked rampant, totally animal. My long, dark blonde hair had gone stringy in the humidity; my eyes were wide and hungry. My breasts, small and pert at the best of times, rode high on my rib cage, nipples hard and primed. A tide of heat was growing visible on the surface of my skin, from groin to neck. My body was on fire, but what was going on in my mind was way worse. I was almost totally out of control, and yet... so in control. That's what this had done to me: this power.

I looked back at Carl and I forgot to be aware of myself, totally. He was struggling with his burden; he was struggling with his need to come. He was so much a victim of my whims. It was that, I realized, that strength contained, that I hungered for. I wanted to feel its potency roar inside me, I wanted to trigger the final release and feel it where it counted most. I threw one leg over his tethered body, straddling his hips, steadying myself with two fingers latched over the rope across his chest. The air rushed between my thighs, over the hot, anxious skin of my hungry pussy.

"That looks so good in your hands," he blurted. He was looking down at my talons, where they bit into the rope. "Oh, yes, that's good," he said, as I flexed my fingers, scratching my nails over his chest. He went to say more, and then his words slipped away and instead, he roared aloud. With one swift gliding action, I had taken him inside.

I was so wet. My inner muscles clasped at his bloated cock. I could feel his balls primed beneath my buttocks when I ground down against his hips. I didn't have long; his face was contorted with ecstasy. I gripped the rope that bound him, and rode him, hard and fast, crushing his cock inside me again and again. The bind of rope along the upper side of his cock added its own pressure and I arched over him, my clit sparking against the surface of the rope, my entire body wired into the multiple stimuli.

"Oh fuck, fuck me," he shouted, rolling his eyes. It was barely perceptible, given his status, but he began to buck his pelvis against his constraints and then his cock lurched and spurted inside me. I grabbed his head in my hands and leaned over, kissing his mouth, crushing my clit on the rope and squeezing his cock hard as he came. Moments later, I threw back my head and roared with my own release.

"You know that handmade bondage rope you mentioned?" I said. Lizzie looked up from her latte and frowned. Georgina's head snapped round, her eyes bright with interest. She knew me; she knew I wouldn't mouth off. "It really is special isn't it?"

Lizzie grinned. I sipped my café negro, whilst winking at Georgiana over the rim of the cup.

"Especially when done with *true style*," I added, smiling, and glanced at my newly manicured fingernails—wine-red, of course, to match Carl's rope. Because it was weeks later and we were still playing. As for my inner sex kitten, I reckon she had become more of a lioness, what with Carl and his rope to toy with, but perhaps I'll let you decide on that score.

Cuffed

Savannah Stephens Smith

I'm not a cop groupie.

So when a man wearing a dark uniform walked into the office at ten minutes after five, a man with more muscle than he needed, a gun, and a deadly serious expression, my initial reaction was nervous guilt. *Oh, no. What did I do?*

Then I remembered that I hadn't done anything, and I was annoyed with myself. And with him, since he'd provoked it. I kept typing—I wasn't the receptionist, and besides, we were closed. It was quiet, almost everyone gone. I ignored him, far from the sort of reaction I could imagine my friend Marianne having in the same situation: *I've been a very bad girl, officer, and I should be taken...into your custody.*

Sometimes we amuse ourselves with quiet comments as we work, however, I mostly keep my quips to myself. Business is business, after all, and I'm not the office comedienne. But it had been a long week, I was working late, and even an imagined witticism was enough to make me laugh. The audible snort that escaped wasn't as contained and controlled as it should have been.

The good-looking man at the reception counter looked over at me, his face a disconcerting blank. And he had those cold eyes. Cold eyes—warm heart? Laughter turned into a sigh. Blame it on springtime. It was 5:15, I was still at work, and I was beginning to think that breaking up with my ex, Brian, hadn't been such a good idea.

Oh, yes, it had. He hadn't been good enough for me, and I knew it. I deserved better. The trouble is, being strong sometimes hurts almost as much as—

"Trouble, miss?"

The cop at the reception counter was looking at me. Where was our receptionist? Gone home, probably. Well, that wasn't my fault. I was the department secretary in the rental part of the office.

"No, no trouble," I said, my face hot. It was none of his business. I went back to what I'd been doing. Typing a tenancy agreement of all things—we were a low-tech office. The agreement had an annoying carbon copy for the tenant. The top page always looked fine (thank goodness for a correction ribbon on the IBM) but the underside was always a mess, with every typo showing through. I peeked discreetly at the cop, the sound of my typing loud in the post-workday quiet. Why didn't he go away?

Very cute. Youngish, maybe thirty-five or so. Dark hair, neatly short. Clean shaven. I couldn't tell what color his eyes were—and it didn't matter, I reminded myself—but they were serious. And there was some serious muscle on him, too. His shoulders strained against the uniform, and he wore that gear they all come equipped with as easily as if it were made of plastic. *Clack, clickity, clack* went the keys of the typewriter. *Click, click,* to backspace and correct. *Clack-clack-clack. Clack*. I peeked again. He was looking at me. Then it hit me, and I felt sick.

My laugh. He thought I was snorting. At him. Snort. Pig.

Cop. Pig.

I spoke before I thought. His eyes were intense, and the office was so quiet. I hated my urgency to apologize, but did it anyway. "Sorry. I was just... It's been a busy day. I didn't mean it that way."

"Mean what?" Nice voice. Low and deep, warm as a furnace's rumble on a December night.

Crap. "Never mind. I'm sorry. Has anyone helped you? I believe...," I gestured to the counter, "they're all gone for the day."

And that's how it started. He was there to pick up keys, so I abandoned the hateful typewriter and searched for them. Up close, he was even more intimidating. The way they wear that uniform sets them apart from the rest of us. As I searched, I explained about the laugh, how busy it had been lately, and that I was working late. "I think stress makes me silly," I apologized.

"I can relate," he said, and smiled. When he smiled, he wasn't so scary. He had a nice smile.

I found the keys. They were propped up in a white envelope with *Congratulations, Eric!* written in a feminine hand. One of the realtors from the sales side. "My house," he said. "Nothing big or fancy, but..." The pride on his face as he held the envelope, shaking it gently and making the keys inside slide back and forth, took away from the menace of his uniform.

"That's great," I said, and meant it.

It turned out that he was looking at me because he thought I was pretty, not because I'd made a pig snort sound. What do you know? But when he asked me out, I declined. I had work to do, and so I closed the door and locked it behind him—I noticed through the window that he waited until the deadbolt turned and clicked before he nodded and walked away with his keys. And his uniform. I went back to the typewriter. I sat down, put my hands on those keys, and noticed that everyone else had long gone, and no one cared if I worked late. I said out loud: "Screw it. I'm going home."

I don't troll for tickets, turned on by a uniform, and I don't hang out in cop bars. Frankly, I've only read about cop hangouts in novels. I'm like most people: when I see that light-bar-on-top silhouette in my rearview mirror, I get a pang in my gut and hit the brakes. Then I drive like a teenager with a brand-new learner's permit and a mother in the backseat. I'm a good girl, and I stay out of trouble. And I'm no slut.

But sometimes things can change a little. The second time Eric asked me out, I said yes.

Eric soon learned I wasn't a cop groupie. I didn't want to hang around with the other wives and girlfriends of his fellow officers—frankly, none of those women were interesting enough for me to give up a good book or my own private time. I'd done my time trying to please a man, doing what I thought he'd want me to do. And be.

I was too old for that nonsense.

But the trouble with cops is that they make you feel guilty—even when you haven't really done anything.

It was a summer afternoon. Eric had moved into his new house, a modest bungalow that needed a little fixing up. By July it was neat, newly painted, and pleasing. I was there, waiting for him to change. He had just come off shift. He had come into the bedroom, dumped most of the gear on the bed, and then gone off again to answer the phone. We were going to go to a barbecue at his sister's place. I was going to meet his parents.

There it was on the bed. The belt, and all the accessories. I thought of that poem, the one about adoring a fascist. Then I decided that it was too nice a day to think about the implications of adoring a fascist, psychosexual complexities, or even modern poetry. Was it Plath? Maybe, Plath and her line about a *brute heart*.

Eric wasn't like that, though—he was a teddy bear who only looked tough. Underneath the uniform was a guy even my mother would like. Despite his work, generally he was sunny and sweet. And underneath the uniform was a man I could, just maybe sometime, love. I waited for him, idly checking my hair.

I turned to leave the bedroom, but glanced back.

The pile of heavy, black...*stuff* laying there was irresistible. The belt was a thick, black snake resting on his bed. So I, with the soul of Eve, checked it out at last. I touched the things Eric used, the tools of his trade. They were things that intimidated, commanded, and subdued. They were cool to the touch and all black. These were things that he handled every day, but they were things that ordinary people—good girls and nice boys—wouldn't know about. We stay out of trouble. Flashlight. A stick. A shiver danced up my arms and down again. Something in a canister. Mace? Pepper spray? We didn't talk about his work much. A pouch with a snap on it. The gun, last, but I didn't touch that. I *wouldn't* touch that. I'm not stupid, and I knew it was loaded. So I went back to the pouch.

I'd opened it and taken out the weighty handcuffs, fascinated. "You want to play, Beth? You think those are toys?" His voice was deadly quiet, but I jumped anyway, like I'd swallowed electricity. I felt that sick clench in the gut, the hot shame of being caught. I was seven again, with cookie crumbs on my mouth and no ready excuses.

"No," I said, jumping up quickly, putting some distance between me and the things I had been, well, playing with. I was surprised by his anger—I hadn't seen him like this. He stepped closer to me, and I babbled further apology. Something else gathered between us, something dark and dangerous, eclipsing all that had ever gone before. Where was the nice guy, my new boyfriend, lover of puppies, springtime, and his toddler nephews?

Gone. Just like the sun behind a cloud. Instead of smiling and forgiving me with a kiss, a kiss I'd been half-expecting, leaning forward with my mouth shaped to kiss back, he grabbed my arm. He spun me around. Suddenly, I was facing his bureau and my right arm was pinned up and behind me. It was held fast in such a way that I knew he could, just as easily as not, break it. I grabbed the dresser for balance. A lamp teetered, a quarter slid off a dime. "Hey!" I said.

That's when he grabbed my other arm and cuffed me. The click of the metal sliding home was loud. The metal was cold and heavy. My mouth was dry. He'd never done anything like this before. Had I been wrong about him?

"This isn't funny," I said.

"And my cuffs aren't toys," he said.

"I'm sorry." I didn't want to apologize, but I thought it was the best thing to say.

"Sorry's not enough. You play with the cuffs, what's next, Beth? The gun?"

"Of course not."

My hands were behind my back, and the cuffs were on me. They were unforgiving. I'd often wondered what it was like to wear them. Now I knew. And I didn't like it.

"Take them off," I said. How dare he abuse his position like this? I tried not to feel something else, something dry and crackling, as it crept up my back. My autonomy was gone, and that was a scary thing. We hadn't been dating long, and maybe I'd made a very bad choice. This wasn't the boyfriend I knew, the guy who I had caught crying at a sad movie we'd seen only two weeks ago.

"No."

"Please." I held my chin up, didn't turn around, playing martyr. I was stubborn, even as I pleaded. I wouldn't look at him. I wouldn't back down, and it seemed neither would he. Stupid fights start like this, over something small that becomes unforgivable.

When you're a woman, and your hands are behind your back, that position does something. It arches your back slightly, pushes your shoulders up—and your breasts out. I was a little disconcerted to feel my nipples hardening, puckering against the cup of my bra. More than that—there was a familiar, warm itch between my legs. It grew hotter, like sun spilling over the horizon.

"I'm sorry," I said again.

Eric didn't take the cuffs off. Instead, he tugged me, and I took a helpless step backward away from the bureau into the center of the room. I didn't like this at all. He walked around and faced me, still in his uniform. I wouldn't look at him. He was treating me like a child, not his girlfriend. I saw my face reflected in his badge. I looked strange, distorted in the metallic surface. I didn't want to know what his face showed. Was it that scary blank expression?

He unbuttoned my blouse, and drew it down over my shoulders. I refused to speak, as if protesting would give him more leverage. He didn't say a word about my nipples being hard. He couldn't remove the blouse completely with me still cuffed, and it dangled off my arms. The light fabric hid them, but I knew they were still there. How could I not? I was only lucky they were not too tight. I wondered who the last person Eric had cuffed had been. What man—

Or *woman*—

It was July, but I shivered. What other women had felt his steel around their wrists? Eric didn't talk. I didn't know what he'd do next. It was the kind of fight when part of the dark appeal of conflict is provoking the other, goading him, pushing things. Stuff that you normally wouldn't say or do rises up, gliding from the dark depths. He didn't back off.

My bra came undone next, the same way. I should have

turned, squirmed to evade his fingers, but I didn't. He pulled it up and lifted it over my head. The air caressed my bare skin. The straps he slid down my arms, chuckling as he stripped me. My breasts were bared and I was helpless.

And aroused.

There was a part of me, a deep and primal part, which bloomed as if it had waited all my life for this afternoon. A late flower, a twenty-seven-year blossom.

The skirt came off next. A simpler piece of clothing one couldn't imagine: a narrow elastic waist and the smooth drop of fabric. It was a summer skirt that I wore a lot that year, slipping it on in the morning over bare legs freshly shaved. I liked the way the skirt swished against my skin, panty hose scorned for summer. I wore a plain black T-shirt with it most days, but that afternoon I'd picked a blouse. I'd never see the skirt hanging in my closet again without its pattern reminding me of this afternoon, reminding me of the way light slanted in at an angle through the closed blinds, the sounds of an ordinary summer afternoon going on outside, and how the handcuffs had become warm from my skin, but still heavy. Still present.

Eric told me to step out of it, and I did. I should have kicked him, but I'd swallowed a two-edged sword: fear and arousal. I didn't know how it would sit in my belly. I still wore my shoes, frivolous summer sandals with a bit of a heel. But this wasn't how I imagined the afternoon progressing when I'd dressed for a barbecue with his family.

I stood there, mulish and naked, dangling my clothes behind my back. I felt small and bad, a naughty child. I wanted to feel his hot tongue rasping over my nipples. I wanted him to stop this. He took my panties down next, slowly, and I didn't feel childlike at all. Cotton slid down my thighs, and I seeped want.

Then I was naked and he was still in uniform, though he wasn't wearing that belt. His uniform was blue, the color of night sky at ten o'clock. Indigo, or something darker. He spoke softly, as softly as the skirt lay on the carpet. "Should I leave you like this, Beth, for the barbecue?" Oh, god. No. A quiver went through me, as I imagined Eric leading me down the steps from the side of the house into his backyard, guiding me as I walked, teetering slightly, without my arms free for balance. As I walked, still cuffed. Still in my sandals. Still naked. Like a prize. His friends, colleagues, men with the same hard faces, the same eyes that had seen so much, there. And now their eyes would rake my naked skin, from mouth to ankle. I trembled, imagining. That scenario was barbaric.

A hot clench of desire shook me. I was getting wet.

"All right." His voice was so gentle that I wanted to cry. That sounded like the Eric I knew—or thought I knew—the one that took moths outside instead of killing them with a brutal smack of a magazine, who loved playing with the neighbor's dog. But there was more to him, I knew now: unexpected corners in his psyche. I should have known it all along. You don't get to be a cop without being tough, without being a bit of a bastard. Even if he was a nice guy. Nice guys had their night sides, too.

"Why don't you kneel, Beth?"

But it wasn't a question. His hand on my cuffed arm held me steady as I sank to the carpet. I wasn't the only one who'd been moved by this game of taunt and dare. I was face to crotch with him, and even though his uniform was dark, the fact that Eric was erect was clear. I could see the outline of his penis, stiff against the fabric. An answering wave of desire rolled through me. Being naked for him turned me on. His zipper went down with an insinuating slide, and I pulsed. I'd be damned if I'd let him know, though.

His warm skin touched my mouth and I opened my lips. I didn't need to be told what to do next. He slid inside, thick, surging upward, and I sucked. It was hard to do without my hands free. I never realized how much I liked to grab the base of his cock and squeeze. How much I liked to have some control over how much, how fast, or how deep he went into my mouth. I liked to play with his balls, heavy, soft and, vulnerable. With my wrists bound behind my back, I sucked. I was helpless, balancing on my knees, the world come down to his flesh against my tongue, his steel on my skin.

I couldn't touch myself. I could squeeze my thighs together, but that jeopardized my balance. I sucked. He swayed, slowly sliding his prick in and out of my mouth. It was absurd, with the sounds of children outside, the thunk-thunk of a basketball against a hoop in the driveway next door. I could hear voices rising, falling. A summer afternoon. I could even smell someone else's barbecue. That's what we were supposed to be doing. We should be getting ready, not playing out this uncivil, ruthless scene. In the dim light, I sucked him, want growing with every stroke along his shaft, every sigh. Ordinary had fled, leaving me on my knees, bound. I felt like a hummingbird, drinking from a flower in the darkness. A slave girl on the market, being tested in a back room.

I felt better than I had in years.

I was wet and aching for touch. I wouldn't tell him, though. The whole thing was outrageous. Surely he must know that this episode would be the end of "us." As soon as I was free, I'd be free of him.

He could smell the lie on me. I could, too: my arousal was in the air like smoke. I sucked him, his skin warm, silky, and rigid. *You like it too*, I thought, shifting on my knees, arms beginning to ache. How long had it been since Eric had spun me around and cuffed me? Ten minutes? Fifteen? An eternity? He'd become hard doing it. He was getting off on this. His erection in my mouth was proof.

My compliance was also proof of something. What, I didn't want to think about.

Only his cock. I sucked, grateful for that contact of skin, something to focus my hunger on. My cunt was engorged, my nipples too, but there were no caresses to slake my want. All I could do was suck, so I did. That, and rub my breasts against his legs like a pet begging for attention. It was degrading. Luckily for me, his uniform trousers were made of a fabric with a bit of stiffness to it. I sucked him for a long time, falling into a rhythm where I could take him in and out without choking, without fear. He didn't speak. It went on until his breathing changed, his hand came to rest on my head, and his body began to tense. I wasn't helpless, then. I could do that to him.

He was close to coming, but he pulled out. I closed my mouth, testing the emptiness, easing my jaw. "Do you like my toys, Beth?"

"No," I lied, truculent. Why didn't he touch my breasts? I was helpless to stroke, and my nipples were hard with yearning.

"Liar." Eric turned away from me, his erection a blunt, fleshy club that protruded, rude and blatant, from his uniform pants. I licked my lips. I wanted that cock again. In me. Deep.

"Arms hurt? Legs?"

"No."

"Lying again." His hands were warm on my rib cage as he lifted me to my feet. He walked around me again, observing me. I didn't know what would happen next, and I'd never felt more naked.

He knelt, his hands on my inner thighs, and opened my legs wider. I almost stumbled, but kept my balance. He leaned in, and deliberately licked at my damp skin. Just once, and I gasped with pent-up want when his hot tongue slid over my pussy. Once. Slowly across my swollen clit—the hard center in a sea of wanton need. That was the cruelest thing, far worse than the handcuffs, far worse than anything. To do it just once. He chuckled again, and rose, his prick still thrusting outward, a baton of a different sort. "What to do with you...," he mused, as if he didn't have a hundred ideas. He pivoted slowly, hand on his chin, pretending to consider the possibilities.

Eric went to the bed and slipped his nightstick from the loop. He wouldn't beat me with it? No. That wouldn't be rational. But fear prickled my flesh again, desire abating for a moment. I thought of something else he could do with it, and another wave of dread washed over me. I didn't want that.

Gently, with calm control, he slid the nightstick against my damp pussy. I gasped at the cool of it. Desire returned. At last, something was touching me. The smooth surface glided along my hot skin. I was panting. I spread my thighs wider and bent my knees to increase the pressure, and rode the wood. Eric chuckled in the dim bedroom, and pressed harder. I whimpered and humped it. I didn't care that all my dignity had gone, flown with the *click* of the cuffs on my wrists. I needed to come. "Please touch my breasts," I whispered, hating myself for voicing it.

He didn't bother acknowledging my request. He touched me when and where he wanted, and all I could do was suffer or enjoy. I was a sweet ache, all skin and nerves. He went back to the bed, and absently stroked his cock, stiff and conspicuous, looking down at his belt and accessories. I swayed, almost dancing, my blouse and bra dangling ridiculously. I wondered what would happen next.

"I can't really use the spray—you're already pretty cooperative, Beth." He considered the flashlight. "And I think you've seen the light." Another low laugh. He picked up the belt. "Sit." I perched on the edge of the bed, legs primly together, just as my wrists remained bound behind me. He knelt before me, and I thought he was going to go down on me now. My knees drifted apart, I tilted my cunt to him. He held up the belt. He stroked my inner thighs with it, the leather cool and heavy, though an entirely different sensation from the cuffs and the baton. Slowly he teased me, tracing patterns on my skin; circling my belly, my thighs, closer and closer to my vulva. He brushed my pubic hair with the belt and I sighed. It felt like wind sounds when it drifts through the tops of the pines at night. I opened my legs wider, throbbing. I could see his prick, swollen, but I couldn't touch him. It was driving me crazy. I closed my eyes.

I felt something nudge me open, but it wasn't his mouth, or his finger. The tip of the leather belt prodded between my labia, going ever deeper. I didn't know what to say. I was wet and Eric crouched before me, intent. Carefully, he pushed the leather belt into my pussy, and I breathed, deep and ragged. I felt dizzy. It was awful and demeaning. It was a terrible taunt: close, but not a cock.

"Is this kinky?" His voice was soft.

I didn't answer. He pushed a little more and I didn't close my thighs or try to stop him. I rocked against the belt, not sure if I was trying to get away from it, or trying to rub my slick pussy against the edge of leather. I craved hot friction. "You like it, Beth," he said. "Don't you?"

"No."

He smiled at the lie. "Stand." Eric unlocked one wrist, my arms dropped to my sides and I sighed with the pleasure of release. I shook off my blouse and bra, shook my tingling arm. Freedom didn't last long; he pushed me back down onto the bed. I was weak and entirely compliant, under the spell of his strangeness. "Lie down."

I did, the bedspread smooth against my skin. He left my shoes on. He took my right arm and cuffed my wrist to the bedpost. I looked up at the blank globe of his overhead light. "Better?"

"Yes." My voice was a grateful mumble.

My spread legs were an invitation one didn't need to be a

cop to decode. Still, he took his time unbuttoning his shirt. I moved, restless against his sheets. I watched Eric undress, the dark uniform falling away, *cop* becoming *man*. Underneath, he was muscular and hairy, and entirely comfortable nude. He sat on the edge of the bed.

He slid a finger down my vulva, my lips opening for him again. He slipped into the wetness up to his knuckle, more easily than the leather belt had. I eyed his cock, springing upward, and the length of his thigh, muscled and downy. He was beautiful. Then Eric was on top of me, a solid weight, his skin all along mine. I reacted with a surge of want, ferocious, pulling him to me with one arm, pulling at the cuff with my other. At last the warm head of his cock touched me. I quivered, and worked my hips up to meet him, to urge him to enter me. I was slick, sticky, and unbearably ready for him.

Slowly, he pushed his cock into me, slippery enticement making it easy. He groaned. My turn to laugh, in triumph. He fucked me, slowly, his cock sliding in and out in long, measured strokes. I fucked him back. With one hand cuffed to the bed, the other on his ass, I wrapped my legs around him tight. I hated him with joy and pleasure.

His voice was a slow, patient whisper as he remorselessly stroked me with his body. "You've—" He thrust in. "Been bad—" And out, his skin a hot embrace. "You know."

"Yes." I rocked with him, faster, and bucked back, my fever rising. I was almost there, the hot friction—

I made a sound as I came, like something hurt. It didn't. Still cuffed, I felt my release come. It rolled over me, lifted me. I soared. "It's for your own good, Beth," he muttered, frantically thrusting. "All for your own good...."

I know.

Oh, I know.

Leered At

Debra Hyde

I remember the first time a grown man leered at me. Not a college student or an early thirty-something, but a real adult, someone my father's age. Someone who should've known better and probably did, but chose to lust after me anyway. It happened the summer before I left for college while I was hanging out at a pool party with my best friend. I'd just turned eighteen. We had wandered in from the pool for the snack table, unaware as we passed the bar that the adults' consumption of highballs had surpassed frat house kegger dimensions.

That's when I noticed my girlfriend's uncle. His face was slack from too much drink, but his eyes had narrowed and a sly grin had crept across his face. Lurid, the look was unmistakably lurid. And it was aimed right at me.

That look—*his* look—was so penetrating that I felt like he knew my every secret—like whether boys had already parted my legs—and it suggested he had his own secrets, like the unsavory possibility that he knew even better than those boys how a man could part my legs. Ultimately, his leer told me that he'd like nothing better than to have a go at me.

I was stunned, instantly humiliated, so ashamed that for the eternity of a split second I froze in a clichéd deer-meets-headlights trance. I blushed so hard, it hurt. I prayed that his niece, my best friend, didn't notice his drunken leer—or my embarrassment. It was all so lump-in-the-throat disturbing and repulsive.

"Meet me outside," I told my girlfriend. I fled the room with, I hoped, some measure of grace to conceal my plight. But my every step felt clumsy, leaden, and weighed down by my shame. I could only assume success because no one questioned my behavior.

In the fresh air of the cool evening, the blush of humiliation faded from my cheeks and my racing heart slowed. But a rush of anger followed on its heels and I grew as livid as that man had been lurid. My anger was so potent, I shook uncontrollably.

There, in the coming darkness of midsummer's eve, I vowed to myself if a man ever leered at me again, I wouldn't let it go uncontested. I'd glare back and stare him down. No one else would ever have the upper hand again.

Or so I thought. In the coming years, my vow would protect me from men but not from my own fantasies. You see, I never forgot his leer and I often recalled the moment I spied it. Then, in the privacy of my fantasies, I enacted my vow and stared him down. My own eyes would narrow; my lips would slip into slyness. I would up the ante rather than diffuse the moment. In my fantasy, we'd slip away so I could reveal to him my brazen and knowledgeable self. In my fantasy, I was forever eighteen, but in real time I was forever aging and my past shame had transformed itself into pure thrill.

If my fantasy became luridly skewed, then my reality grew downright warped. I developed a preference for older men, starting with college professors and, later, on-the-job superiors. I wasn't bucking for the dean's list or top-notch performance appraisals; I could earn those on brains and merit alone. I wanted them because I lusted for the raw power of an older man, one willing to foist his sexual prowess on younger flesh. And I craved being that younger flesh.

I craved Daddy fucks.

But now that I've reached forty, finding a good Daddy fuck isn't that easy. It's hard to find savvy older men who can look beyond the middle-aged woman to see the inner girl, to find men who don't apply the strict numeric standard of "27 and under" in defining *girl.*

Funny, really, because younger men often look my way, hoping to catch my gaze and interest. Sure, young hunks crave an older woman's worldly experience but however trendy MILFs might be right now, younger men were never credible candidates to me.

Ironically, the Uncle Leer of My Ages Past was. Or so I discovered several months ago, at a cocktail party.

It was one of those business soirées where your vendor woos you like some smarmy Victorian suitor, plying you with promises and hints of good things to come if only you'd let him cop a quick feel. I had just slipped a tip into the barkeep's cup and, drink refreshed, turned toward the client-based crowd.

And there he was: Uncle Leer, older now and totally sober if his seltzer water was any indication, chatting up a colleague. As age is likely to make a person, he was heavier, his hair thinner and gray, but time hadn't changed those subtle movements you never forget. He was instantly recognizable.

Somehow, he sensed my dumbfounded stare and, catching me, cocked his head in a "do I know you?" manner. I smiled slyly—without leering, of course—and issued a teasingly nonverbal "try me."

Soon enough, I had my chance. As our second, late-night

dinner date concluded, I challenged him, leer and all, on the veranda at an Italian restaurant. Alone, we kissed and, in close embrace, I brought my leg up to his hip. Instinctively, he reached for my thigh, slipped his hand under my skirt, and caressed my panty-less rump.

"Try me, Daddy," I invited.

He would—often, in fact.

Widowed, Daniel still lives in the same ranch-style home of leer past. Initially, it felt odd to revisit the home of the man who had first humiliated me, the man who had unknowingly inspired my private fantasies and my real-life thrills, but now I craved Daniel's upper hand, especially after falling in lust with his frequent erections. So when he messaged me—*Girl, in my study. Over the desk. 6:00 p.m., pronto.*—I went.

There I waited, bent slightly at the waist and leaning forward, hands propped on the desktop, legs spread. The position, the waiting, the anticipation, all made my cunt ready for action. Impatiently, it throbbed and threatened to go wet at the least provocation.

The longer I waited, the more my senses buzzed, heightened and aware, and when Daniel finally approached me, the sound of the den door shutting and locking, the rustle of his clothes as he neared, the pace of his breathing, even the scent of his aftershave, all of it blared in my senses. It was as if my awareness was predicated on his presence.

He was behind me, lifting my skirt. When I felt his warm hands caressing, I knew he was admiring my naked ass.

"My daughter's coming over in a while with the grandkids. Let's hope she isn't early."

I shuddered at the thought. Who knew where he'd have me if she did arrive early. Mid-orgasm? Mid-fuck, even? The possibilities worried me because I wasn't exactly the world's quietest fuck.

Daniel came around to the front of his desk and reached down. A discreetly hidden wrist cuff chained somewhere to his desk appeared in his hand. He drew it tight around my wrist.

My captivity had commenced.

As my other wrist and both ankles felt a similar grip, my legs spread just shy of uncomfortably wide, I quivered. The unforgiving hold of bondage always made me aware of just how completely I had given myself over to him.

I stood, leaning forward just enough so Daniel could access whatever he needed of me, hands on the desk but chains taut enough that I had little leverage. Already my wrists complained about my forward weight and I wondered how long I could maintain this position.

Daniel came behind me again and resumed caressing my ass. I knew how inviting a sight I was—bound, skirt hiked high, my rump and slit exposed—when Daniel leaned against me and pressed his erection against my ass. His breath heated my neck, as if he was a wild animal at my back. My cunt throbbed, telling me to respond and press back into him. I did, moaning and wanting it.

"My housekeeper must think I'm nuts," he said.

What? What did his housekeeper have to do with me? It was an odd non sequitur to come from him and it drew me up short.

"All these years," he explained, "she paid careful attention to this space, knowing how to dust around depositions and briefs and legal journals, just so. And then I told her not to bother anymore. I claimed I had really retired, after all this time."

He nibbled my ear and murmured, "Maybe I should just tell her the truth—that every week, a perfectly fuckable girl stops by, gets tied down, and takes it from behind, right here in this room."

I whimpered, not so much at that unlikely scenario, but because he might really brag as much to fellow legal beagle retirees about his fucktoy. It took no stretch of my imagination to envision him talking about my willing cunt while lounging poolside with the old boys at the country club.

Daniel kissed and nibbled his way around my neck. He stroked my long hair out of the way, then reached forward. He cupped and caressed my breasts, then slowly popped open the buttons on my blouse. He nibbled my neck until, last button undone, he pulled my blouse over my head and let it drop to my cuffed wrists. He returned to my breasts, this time kneading them earnestly. We both moaned as he circled each nipple, as he pinched and stretched them. Again I quivered, which prompted Daniel to jab his still-clothed cock against my backside yet again. I groaned, hoping he'd impale me right then and there and put me out of my aroused misery.

But he relinquished his hold on me instead and came around to the front of his desk. He opened its center drawer, a drawer that no longer held the tools of his trade but now held the temptations of his perversion. I never knew what might emerge from that drawer—a crop, a paddle, a pussy whip—but whatever he chose, I knew I would fall prey to its testing and taunting.

This time, nipple clamps appeared, flat and broad things, tipped with black rubber and connected by a chain lead. They weren't the meanest clamps ever made, but I moaned at the sight of them, knowing they could hurt and arouse. I awaited them with mixed expectations.

Wordlessly, Daniel leaned forward, grabbed a nipple and deftly placed the clamp around it. My breath caught in my throat as the initial pain melted into unmistakable bliss. Just as deftly, he put the other clamp in place. The economy of his movements seemed routine, objectifying, and I faded a bit, the way I always do when he plays with me like I'm some toy, some amusement. Any thought of struggling against my bondage in protest evaporated in the haze of this endorphin surge.

Daniel laughed. He knew my responses well. He picked up the lead that hung between my breasts and found its center. I stiffened and braced myself for his pull. When the clamps bore down on me, I cried out through gritted teeth and arched my back. I tried to stomp my foot, but the bondage rendered my protest pointless.

"What? Does that hurt?" he taunted. "I thought you could stand more. In fact, I know you can."

He pulled the lead as far off to one side of my body as possible, contorting the direction of my hanging tits. Pain twisted through them and I begged for his mercy. Daniel pulled to the other side and I struggled so much that the chains scraped against the fine finish of his desk. A rush of meek, frantic pleas—"Oh please, oh please"—issued from me, but Daniel knew better than to listen.

"Your mouth says 'mercy' but I know what you're really thinking," he teased.

"You don't want mercy. Do you?"

He pulled the lead in the opposite direction.

"No, of course not. That's not what you're thinking."

The lead moved again, still twisting and contorting.

"Tell me what you're really thinking."

I squirmed through it all. Like percussion, the chains that held me rattled where they could or thumped dully against the carpet where they couldn't. My struggle grew not just because of the clamps' severity, but because I knew what he wanted to hear. I knew what he wanted me to admit. But I couldn't utter the words. My mouth gaped like a fish, but the words just wouldn't come.

"Mute? You're mute?" he cried, astonished. "You need some encouragement, I see."

He pulled straight and although the pain no longer twisted

through me, it continued apace and, weary, I began to lose my battle against it.

"Yes, let me help you," Daniel offered, his voice anything but charitable.

He pulled the lead even more, making the clamps bite deeper still. My torment shot upward, at once wretched and wonderful.

"You don't want mercy. At least not mercy from these clamps. Do you?"

The fire in my tits blazed as he pulled. I gritted my teeth and whimpered through my teeth. Still, I couldn't speak.

Daniel continued his steady, unrelenting pull, as much in words as in actions.

"You want mercy all right. You want—"

He pulled so hard the clamps tore from my tender nipples. I bellowed as their release stung me.

"You want a mercy fuck, don't you? Don't you? Admit it! You want me to take you right now and shove my cock up that hole of yours, don't you?"

When the clamps tore from my nipples, Daniel tore whatever resolve I had to shreds.

"Yes! Yes, I do! I want you to fuck me!"

Daniel went behind me. It seemed like he towered over me, me with my burning tits and ready cunt. I heard him unzip his pants. They fell to the ground, pocket contents jangling. Access was a footstep away, ensured by my ensnarement.

Step up to me. Please, step up to me, I silently begged.

Daniel did. I felt his cock brush against me, but its hard touch was fleeting. His hand, however, was a different matter. It grabbed me between the legs, cupping my pussy the way it had earlier cupped my breasts.

"No," I heard. "Not yet."

Daniel's words made me admit defeat. I abandoned the semi-upright position I had held for so long and collapsed over the desk, sending the chains slack and noisy. If I could have wept in frustration, I would have, but Daniel's straying finger found my clit and bliss thwarted me. Rubbing, pressing, coaxing, he gave me pleasure so incredible and so luscious that I went as slack-jawed as some addict drifting in aimless opiate pleasure. But I was not to stay there.

A bright and burning smack sounded across my ass and demanded my attention. More smacks followed and the sweet burn of one escalated into the agonizing sting of many. I moved from meek whimpers to outright cries, unable to distinguish lust from pain. I screamed, out of dismay, out of arousal, out of pain.

Daniel forced a hand over my mouth.

"Remember my daughter might arrive any moment."

Yet still he smacked me. I squirmed to escape him, just inches really, but enough to signal I couldn't take any more. It didn't matter. Daniel didn't stop until my cheeks were ember red. Then he caressed my ass gently, just like in the beginning, and it made me want him all over again.

Even then, he wasn't done toying with me. He grabbed my burning cheeks and spread them, stretching and exposing my asshole. I could sense his cruel delight at having me any way he wanted, but I prayed for his cock elsewhere, where I needed it so desperately. He let go of my asscheeks and brushed his fingers against my slit. Sticky juices smacked as my lips parted to accommodate him, and the sound of my own wetness and his sudden intrusion startled me.

"What a ready little thing you are," Daniel clucked. "Could it be you're expecting to get fucked, dear girl?"

A whimper was all I could squeeze from my lips.

"Oh you can do better than that, my dear," he chided. His fingers left me, one settling on my clit. He leaned into me again, his breath on my neck, and spoke. "Better fess up, better tell Daddy what you need."

I moaned, my cunt convulsed, hinting at what it would give him if only he'd work that clit. His finger heeded its promise and they conspired against me, that cunt and my Daddy.

"Maybe you just need to come once and I can consider my work done."

My cunt spasmed, demanding I answer his question. It wanted the satisfaction of cock and it didn't want me ruining things. I obeyed and confessed.

"No, Daddy, no! Coming won't be enough!"

"What will be enough?" he coaxed. "What will make you a happy little girl?"

He pressed harder into me, thrumming my clit faster. I felt my cunt tighten, then gush. I was irrevocably wet. My cunt, I knew, was swelling, readying itself.

"What do you want, little girl? Tell me."

Daniel's voice grew demanding now, matching my cunt's insistence. How well they worked against me, I thought as I exploded into a deep, prolonged orgasm. And as I fell from that precipice, Daniel cupped my sex in his hand and squeezed. Hard.

"Tell me!"

The agony of his hand wrenched the very last of my reserve. I pulled against my bondage and screamed, "Cock, Daddy! I want cock!" Keyword uttered, my admission was voiced and I collapsed across the desk one last time.

"Cock? You want cock?"

Daniel planted a hand on my hip and aimed at my swollen slit. He pushed hard, refusing any resistance from my body, and satisfied, my cunt delivered its soul to the devil that was my Daddy. It yielded fully.

"Here's your cock, girl."

He took me with slow, methodical strokes, and as he did he felt huge, fierce, relentless. But soon enough, his pace escalated until a moan signaled his peak and in deep, stabbing thrusts, he came. But it was all too quiet and much out of character. Where had his loud and ferocious self gone? Curious, I looked over my shoulder.

He was leering at me. Lips curled just short of a smirk, eyes narrow and discerning, his face bore that same selfish desire I had seen decades ago, and it was as thrilling to witness in real life as it had been to imagine it in all those years of fantasizing. But the sight of it made me wilt and I realized that my vow, the one I made so long ago, had now shattered completely. And as Daniel pulled out of me, moaning and shuddering, I realized I wanted to be like my vow, nothing if not broken.

All because of a leer.

On Top of the World

Thomas S. Roche

The guests had stayed late, which is why Stephanie and Aidan found themselves on the rooftop patio at two in the morning, drinking Australian Shiraz and listening to *Doctor Hot Sax's Late-Night Bop Hour* on the jazz station. It was a gorgeous night, pleasantly warm on the roof but sweltering down in the apartment. They had brought up a blanket when they decided to stay up—but it was warm enough that they didn't need it, and the blanket stayed neatly folded on one of the spare chairs. The faint sounds of city traffic could be heard far below, but the rest of the building was somber as a church. Buildings stretched as far as the eye could see—lofts, office buildings, and high-rise apartments, most of them lower than the newly renovated apartment building, which meant that the whole city was presented in a panorama of urban sprawl. This far downtown, most of the buildings went dark at night, so you could even see the stars, spinning overhead in a great ballet, one that became decidedly more spinny whenever Stephanie put her head back and looked up.

"I shouldn't have had that last glass of wine," she said woozily, staring up and puffing on one of the usually forbidden American Spirits that always seemed to come out when the wine flowed. When she looked back down, Aidan had a wicked smile on his face and a pair of handcuffs dangling from one outstretched finger.

"But I'm kind of glad you did," he said, and winked at her.

Stephanie had to stifle her natural nervous giggle, a skill she had learned after law school when she started taking depositions. It had bled over into her private life, but the wine had suppressed it somewhat, so a tiny sound escaped, something closer, perhaps, to a chuckle crossed with a titter crossed with a faint, ever so slightly enraptured moan.

"What do you think you're going to do with those?" she asked.

"Get up against the fence and find out," said Aidan, standing up.

Stephanie knew the fence he was talking about; it rested along the edge of the rooftop patio, the place where residents—drunken residents—seemed most likely to lean over, lose their footing, and plunge twelve stories to set off some poor street-parker's car alarm in a dramatic demonstration that Darwinism was alive and well. Made of square black steel bars, it curved inward about six feet above the floor of the patio, its topmost rail creating the perfect place to secure a pair of handcuffs—something Aidan had commented on just the week before, when they'd moved in. At the time, a shiver had gone through Stephanie, but it was only one week and half a bottle of Shiraz later that it actually seemed like a good idea.

Her eyes lingered on the railing with the hint of trepidation that told Aidan, immediately, that she was going to do what he said. Still she played coy, though, part of their game.

"All the neighbors could see," she said.

"They're either sleeping or horny," said Aidan. "Guess which one I am?"

"You're serious?" said Stephanie, a faint smile playing at the edges of her lips. Aidan plucked the American Spirit from between her fingers, took a drag, and dropped it to the patio. He crushed it under his foot and jerked his eyes toward the railing.

"You tell me," he said, and Stephanie melted under that hot gaze.

"Is that a dare?"

"No," smiled Aidan, rattling the cuffs as they dangled from his finger. "Just a very, very firm suggestion."

She rose, only a little unsteady; now that she wasn't looking up, she barely felt drunk at all. She could feel the heat between her legs as, barefoot—having doffed her shoes long ago to enjoy the warm radiance of the sun-baked concrete patio—she sauntered over to the railing and pressed herself against it, arms over her head, clutching the top bar.

"Your move, mister," she said, cocking her body just so and feeling the cool night wind blow through her white silk blouse.

Aidan followed her, seizing one wrist and locking the cuff around it. He smoothly flipped the chain over the bar and cuffed Stephanie's wrists over her head. Then he seized her hair with one hand and kissed her, hard, his tongue exploring her quivering mouth as his other hand found the top of her blouse and yanked.

In that instant before he pulled her shirt open, Stephanie had been afraid her mouth might taste too much like cigarettes for Aidan's liking—that puff he'd taken didn't match the five decadent cigarettes she'd drunkenly sucked down between sips of Shiraz and raunchy conversations with their dinner guests. But at the moment he began to undress her like that—fiercely, almost violently—she forgot just about everything except the heat between them.

She had half expected him to undress her like this—top first, exposing her breasts—but not with such ferocious disregard for her sixty-dollar blouse. The buttons popped free so that one hit the concrete patio and rolled; she could hear another clinking wetly into a wineglass somewhere, still a third clanking on the metal patio table. The sweat-moist silk that came free from her body, Aidan's heat against her as he pressed his body to hers and pinched one nipple through her lace bra—it all combined in a swirl that made her totally incapable of doing anything except moaning softly into his mouth and melting into his arms.

When his tongue withdrew, however, she managed to whimper a breathless plea—disguised as a question.

"Are you sure this is a good idea?" she asked.

Aidan's eyes turned wolfish in that way they did when he was about to fuck her just the way she wanted. "I think it's a fucking great idea," he said, and kissed her again, deeper, pinching her nipple harder. Stephanie squirmed against him, sensations in her nipple mingling as pain, pleasure, pain, pleasure, pain—and then his hand slid just a few inches over, enough to work the front clasp on her bra with one simple movement of middle finger, forefinger, and thumb, faster than Stephanie herself would have been able to do it.

The thin lace of her white bra came peeling away from her breasts, the night air cooling them as the sweat evaporated in what felt like wispy swirls of vapor. Her nipples hardened immediately, even more than they had when Aidan had started pinching them. They hardened so much that it hurt—until Aidan's mouth moved down quickly and enveloped one firm bud, his tongue flicking rhythmically across it as Stephanie whispered, "Jesus!"

Her next sound was anything but a whisper—and the sound of Charlie Parker did little to camouflage the moan that erupted from her lips when Aidan began to tongue and pinch her nipples faster. She wriggled against him, grasping the bar as he mercilessly worked both of her nipples, one pinched between thumb and forefinger, the other suckled deep into his mouth. Her eyes roved wildly, windows spinning everywhere. There were a lot of apartments in the twelve-story building. One of their neighbors could decide to come out onto the patio for a late-night smoke. Some crazy young executive could decide to drop by one of the offices across the way, late on a Saturday, to pick up some papers; someone in one of the apartments opposite them could be hanging out in his living room and pull a Jimmy Stewart on her. Any one of them could see her—witness the details of her surrender. She opened her mouth to beg Aidan to stop—someone could see.

Then Aidan drew away from her breasts, a string of his spittle glistening in the moonlight, and reached for her belt.

The plea for him to stop never came—instead, she uttered a helpless moan as he undid the buckle and pulled her flared silk slacks quickly over thighs, letting them fall to her bare ankles. Stephanie pressed her thighs together, twisting her hips to one side, her body resisting instinctively even as Aidan knelt down, hooked his arm under her thighs, and lifted her just far enough to sweep her slacks out of the way.

Her blouse and bra open, her slacks gone, Stephanie stood with only her thong covering her, the cool night air reminding her with every tingle of her flesh that she was all but naked, here at the top of the world.

Kneeling still, Aidan looked up at her, firmly opening her thighs and licking his way up their insides, then lingering on her belly so that his tongue traced circles around her pierced navel. Before, Aidan's body had partially hidden her front; she had felt less exposed. Now, her bared breasts were revealed for any voyeur out there to see, and the feel of that made her nipples harden more and her cunt go liquid as Aidan slipped his hands under the waistband of her thong and pulled the soaked slip of lace swiftly down her thighs.

When her thong was around her ankles, Stephanie stared into Aidan's upturned eyes, recognizing the fire in them and the twisted smile on his face. Anyone could be watching. They should stop. They should really, really stop.

Then she lifted one foot and stepped out of her thong, letting Aidan open her legs as his mouth descended between them.

His tongue slipped between her swollen lips as his strong arms lifted her thighs onto his shoulders. Aidan had broad shoulders; it was one of the things she liked most about him, physically speaking. She'd never really noticed how perfectly spaced they were to serve as supports for her thighs while he went down on her. Then his tongue found her clit, and the biomechanics of her thighs were the furthest thing from her mind—there was another kind of biomechanical equation that concerned her far more, and Aidan applied it with rhythmic strokes of his tongue, making Stephanie shudder and thrust her head back, through the bars of the railing—so there was nothing between her and the sky as she stared up, moaning unselfconsciously.

Two fingers slid easily into Stephanie's cunt, the pads of them finding her G-spot as Aidan's tongue quickened on her clit. She shivered all over as the cold night air met the rising heat of her almost-naked body. Aidan thrust in deeper and reached up to pinch her nipple as Stephanie mounted toward a quick, unexpected orgasm.

She writhed in the air, her hands gripping the bar and her thighs supported on Aidan's shoulders. With her head thrust back through the wide spaces in the railing, she felt like she was floating in space. She could see lights in windows of the nearby buildings. She could feel phantom eyes watching her. Aidan's hand moved from one breast to the other, working each nipple in a rhythm that matched his tongue on Stephanie's clit and his fingers against her G-spot. She was on the edge, and he could tell—would have been able to tell, even if she hadn't long ago given up being quiet and released herself into wild sounds of ecstasy, her throat aching with the cries she uttered as she closed in on her climax.

Then his fingers came out of her, his tongue left her clit, and he was up, positioning her knees over his shoulders, leaning into her so that her own shoulders pressed hard against the railing—so hard it hurt, not that she cared. Aidan got his pants open and worked his hard cock up the drenched length of her slit, teasing her clit just enough before fitting his cockhead into her entrance. Then he slid into her, and she cried out louder than ever as the sensations took her.

Stephanie came in the first few thrusts, hovering in space, feeling Aidan's hand thrust between the bars and then twisting in her hair to keep her from hitting her head on them. She shuddered as her climax exploded through her, and Aidan's deep soundings brought her orgasm higher, pushing her further with each thrust as he let out a moan and came inside her. She flooded hot and wet with his juice, feeling his mouth on her neck, sucking hungrily as his movements slowed and eased up.

When he withdrew, Stephanie was the one panting, her thighs too unsteady to hold her. He had the key ready, and unfastened the cuffs with one hand before catching her neatly to guide her over to a padded deck chair. She curled up in it, pressing her thighs together to shroud her liquid cunt as Aidan wrapped the blanket around her, the soft acrylic brushing her nipples so that she shivered.

Stephanie's eyes flickered around at the surrounding buildings—seeking the eyes that had captured her, if any actually had. The idea of them—whether they were there or not—made her heart pound faster than the jazz rhythms still pulsing from the radio. She looked up at Aidan, who bent down and kissed her.

"How do you feel?" he asked.

She clutched his hand to her shoulder and smiled.

"On top of the world," she sighed. "On top of the fucking world."

Cropped

Greg Wharton

The air is thick with the scent of damp earth from this morning's weekly watering of the jungle of houseplants. Buffy bathes, and the bright California Sunday afternoon sun streams in onto his orange feline body through the bedroom window.

He stops his grooming for a moment, focusing his gaze up and over the end of the metal bedpost to his humans on the bed, but quickly loses interest in their Sunday games and rolls over to warm his furry stomach in the bright stream of light.

With a hiss the riding crop comes down again on Tony's balls.

SNAP!

"So beautiful..."

And then again twice, this time against the underside of Tony's deep red and painfully hard cock.

SNAP! SNAP!

"Ah... What an angel. Look at that porn-star dick!"

SNAP!

Tony is in his favorite position: on his back in the middle

of their queen-sized bed, his legs pulled back into an extreme *V* over his head, ankles cuffed and snugly roped to the top corner posts. He's naked except for a pair of socks, still damp from the run they took together earlier. This splayed-wide position leaves his cock and balls available to Shane's administrations and his asshole stretched open and ready for any abuse he's so hoping will come.

SNAP! SNAP!

The crop slaps twice on his upper belly just above the spot where his cock points, then grazes up his chest to his nipples, first one and then quickly the other—each adorned with two small plastic clamps—and taps them none too gently, causing a bright flash of pain and an angry yellow light to explode in Tony's vision.

Though he is completely secured by his ankles, Tony's arms are free. It took some time to get used to the personal restraint he has to show, not instantly cringing and flailing his arms when something happens. But he knows that Shane takes great pleasure in watching his eager bottom writhe under his firm and talented hand, and even greater pleasure—being a true Sadist through and through—in the fact that Tony has to control his own arms and hands while being tortured. So Tony learned to let the energy from the endorphins roll out in waves from his arms that lay flat on either side of his body, much like a gymnast would use them for balance, and only occasionally do they even grip at the flannel sheets when the urge to flail them becomes too great. He then stretches out his fingers, letting the release of control and the resulting energy fight any panic.

"Come on, baby. Don't hold back, Tony. You know what I love the most. Make some noise, beautiful man."

Shane's deep brown eyes drill into his.

SNAP! SNAP! SNAP! up the underside of his right leg...

"AH...oh oown oown... AEE—"

Then quickly *SNAP! SNAP! SNAP!* down his left.

"AE AE AE... Aaaaaaaah... FUCK!"

SNAP! sounds the crop on his right asscheek, then *SNAP!* on his left. Trying his best to breathe deep and full, readying for what is coming, he nonetheless holds his breath and bites down hard on his bottom lip when it comes.

SNAP! SNAP! SNAP!

As Shane crops his asshole the endorphin waves start to roll in earnest. Tony can only focus on specific details: the brilliant red color of the roses on the bedside table Shane had delivered to him this morning along with fresh pumpkin muffins and the Sunday paper; the silver and turquoise of the ring on his lover's wide hand that firmly holds the shiny black riding crop now buzzing with so much psychic energy that it leaves colorful trails, as if he were doing acid; Shane's full pink lips and brilliant white teeth as he sneers and smiles to show his pure pleasure and enjoyment.

Tony takes a long, deep breath. He smells the wet houseplants, the roses, the newsprint from the Sunday paper. He smells Shane, whose body gives off a scent like no other when excited and relieving Sadistic urges or delivering pleasure. And he smells himself: his funky, sweaty feet; his own acidic scent that comes with pain and pleasure; and he smells his own asshole. His own asshole's ripe and consuming scent—though he would never admit it to anyone but his lover Shane—that turns him on immensely.

He tries to lift his ass higher, but the position leaves very little movement capability.

"That's it, love. Who's my ass slut? Come on...tell me. Tell me!"

SNAP!

"I am!"

SNAP!

"What do you feel?"

His body heats up, every inch of his skin crackling with electricity, his asshole awash in sensations he is unable to clearly describe. And Shane knows he has difficulty defining it, which gives him even more pleasure in asking him to.

"Baby, I need you. Please fuck me. Now...please... Don't make me talk, fuck me, I can't—"

SNAP!

Shane lays the crop on the bed next to Tony's head, and dips his face to Tony's aching asshole, lapping and tonguing the hot pucker, and groaning deeply like a hungry beast over its kill. He then floats—or so it seems to Tony from his position—off the bed. He gently picks up Buffy and places him in the hall, closing the door. He then lifts, from its hook on the wall, the soft leather blindfold and fits it over Tony's head.

And while Buffy whines and meows many hours too early for his dinner outside their bedroom door, Tony hears the familiar sound of the bottle of lube opening, then feels the cool wetness as it's squeezed into his still hot and stinging asshole. All other sensations melt away when he feels his lover's thick cockhead begin to probe; all is now focused on his asshole and Shane's hard cock. And as the cock slides in, slowly but without any hesitation, his vision of blackness behind the blindfold soon explodes into bright white.

Girls in the Hood

Jolie du Pré

Doneshia and Chavale were almost there. They cut through a lot with grass growing up through cracks in its pavement and strewn with broken glass and paper scraps. A cluster of idle men, languid, with bloodshot eyes from too much drink, leaned against the dented, rusted cars that sat in the center. *Damn cars been here forever*, Doneshia thought.

"Aay, come over here a minute!" one man yelled.

Doneshia took Chavale's hand. "We ain't interested!" she yelled back.

One more block of apartment buildings until Chicago Avenue. The one on the corner was abandoned, but you could often hear faint voices inside.

"Come on, girl!" Doneshia said to Chavale as they crossed Chicago.

Tyrell was on the other side standing with Reigus and Mike.

"Hey, Ty," Doneshia said, pulling Chavale close to her.

"Hey, where y'all goin'?" asked Tyrell.

"To the store."

"Why don't you give me a couple dollars? I'll pay you back."

"I ain't givin' you shit! You always askin' for money."

Tyrell looked at Chavale. "Well, damn, you got any money, baby?"

Reigus and Mike laughed. Doneshia nudged Chavale's side and Chavale stood quiet.

"Why don't she talk? She dumb or somethin'?" Reigus asked.

"I don't know, but she fine as hell ain't she? What's your name, shorty?" Mike asked.

"Her name is Chavale and she don't want your funky ass!" Doneshia yelled, grabbing Chavale's arm. "Fuck y'all, we gone!"

"Go get me a pop and a bag a them chips I like," Doneshia ordered Chavale once inside the store. "Walk slow so I can check that ass."

Chavale smiled shyly, looking over at the Chinese man behind the register, wondering if he had heard. She strolled over to the aisle swinging her generous behind under a snug, short skirt. When she got to the chips, she bent over slowly, reaching for a bag on the bottom shelf. She turned to look at Doneshia, who smiled wickedly at the sight of her tight cheeks peeking out from under the hem. Then Doneshia pointed at the sodas. Chavale held the bag of chips in her hand and sashayed over to the fridge. After they'd paid for the snacks and left the store, they continued on to Doneshia's parents' apartment.

Doneshia had first met Chavale when they were both sixteen, in high school. It was 95 degrees and Doneshia had been sitting in the back of the class, ignoring the teacher, fanning her dark, chubby body with her papers. In walked Chavale, the new girl. Every boy in class stared at the pale-brown beauty with the wavy, black hair, and so did Doneshia. But when Chavale took her seat, she gazed at Doneshia, oblivious to the other stares. Even at sixteen, Doneshia knew she'd fuck her.

Now Doneshia was twenty-two and out of the closet with Christian parents who didn't approve of her homosexuality. But they were gone for the day. She'd sneak Chavale in, like she always did, and they wouldn't know a damn thing.

"Go stand in my bedroom," Doneshia ordered.

"Can I have some chips?" Chavale asked.

"I didn't say you could speak. You speak when I tell you to."

Chavale put her hands on her hips. "This game don't make no sense!" she shouted.

"Look, girl, you open your mouth again and you'll see what you get!"

Chavale looked at the floor, hesitated a moment, and then slunk into the bedroom.

Doneshia smirked. "That's right—go on in there." She carried the soda and the bag of chips and followed behind Chavale, taking a seat on the edge of her bed.

"Take them clothes off nice and slow and I want you to look at me when you do it."

Chavale blushed, with a shy smile, her face also flushed with heat. Doneshia felt that same heat between her legs.

The shoes came off first and then Chavale removed her skirt. She wore no panties and she was shaven. Doneshia had done it, even though Chavale protested the entire time. "I ain't tryin' to fight through all that damn hair," Doneshia had announced as she glided the razor over Chavale's pubes. Now, when Chavale pulled her top off, her large bare breasts bounced in freedom.

Doneshia looked at Chavale's naked body in silence for a moment. "That's nice, real nice," she said softly. "You can talk now. You want some chips?"

"Yes."

"Yes, what?"

"Yes, mister."

"Say 'yes, mistress.' I ain't no mister!"

"I'm sorry—yes, mistress."

"That's better. Now come over here and get some."

Chavale hurried over to Doneshia. "Open your mouth," Doneshia ordered.

Chavale opened her mouth and Doneshia pulled a chip out of the bag and placed it gently onto Chavale's tongue. She munched on it slowly, staring into Doneshia's eyes.

"Pop?" Doneshia asked.

"Yes, mistress."

She opened the bottle and placed it against Chavale's lips. Chavale took a sip and then Doneshia lost control and pulled Chavale close, pushing her hand into her fleshy ass, kissing her hungrily on the lips. Chavale ground her pubic bone and pressed her generous breasts against Doneshia's plump body. But then Doneshia pushed Chavale off.

"That's enough!" Doneshia said. "Now sit down!" Chavale sighed and slumped onto the bed.

Doneshia walked over to her closet and opened it. Chavale watched as she rummaged for something way in the back. She emerged with a sealed brown box.

"What you get?" Chavale asked.

"It's somethin' I ordered off the Internet," Doneshia said as she placed the box on the bed, pulling the tape off. "My momma almost opened this shit. It came when I wasn't home." She reached into the box and pulled several items out.

Chavale's brown eyes grew wide. "What's that?"

"They hoods. We puttin' 'em on."

"I ain't wearin' that!" Chavale said, rolling her eyes in defiance.

"What you mean you ain't wearin' it? You do what I say, remember?"

"They scary lookin'."

"No they ain't. This the one I wear and this the one you wear, 'cause you my slave."

"I ain't no slave!"

"Hush!" Doneshia shouted. "Now put it on like I tell you to!"

"Yes, mistress!" Chavale said sarcastically.

Doneshia shot her a look and Chavale lowered her head.

"Say it and mean it," Doneshia commanded.

"Yes, mistress."

"Good, now put it on."

"How?"

"What you mean, how? Just put the shit on!" Doneshia took her own black hood and pulled it over her head. There were holes in the leather for her eyes, and the front of the mask stopped above her nose and mouth, allowing her to breathe freely.

Chavale giggled and then put her hands over her mouth.

"Stop laughing, girl," Doneshia said, trying to suppress her own laugh. "Put it on."

"It smells funny," Chavale said as she pulled her hood over her face. Hers was similar to Doneshia's, except that her eyes were covered.

"That's 'cause the leather's new, that's all."

"I don't like this. I can't see nothin'."

"I don't want you to see. Now lie on the bed and don't talk."

Doneshia returned to her closet and searched around again.

Chavale sat up abruptly. "What you fixin' to do?"

"I'm gonna put somethin' over your mouth if you don't shut up, girl."

Doneshia walked back over to her bed holding four short pieces of clothesline. She grabbed one of Chavale's hands and started to tie it to the headboard.

"What you...?"

"Hush!" Doneshia shouted.

Chavale kept quiet as Doneshia tied her other hand and her feet to the bed. Then Doneshia climbed on top of her. She put her lips against Chavale's neck and felt a vein there throbbing with nervousness and anticipation. The sight of Chavale wearing a hood made Doneshia gush. Just like the pictures on the Internet, this turned her on. As soon as she got some more money, she'd order more stuff. She liked this game.

Doneshia ran her tongue down Chavale's neck and to her breasts until it danced over her large nipples. Chavale moaned.

"Shhh," Doneshia said.

Then Doneshia pushed her face into Chavale's stomach, sticking her tongue in and out of her navel. This made Chavale giggle, but this time Doneshia didn't quiet her. She brought her tongue to Chavale's mound and Chavale squirmed and bucked. She knew what Chavale wanted. She wanted it too.

"You can talk again," Doneshia said. "Who do you love?"

"You," Chavale said. "I love you."

Doneshia flicked her tongue at Chavale's hard clit. Her juices were so heavy they were smeared along the insides of her thighs. Her sweet musk permeated the room. Doneshia was wet too. By now her panties and even her pants were soaked. But she kept her clothes on.

"What you want me to do, eat your cootchie?"

"Yes!"

"Yes, what?"

"Yes, mistress."

Doneshia dived into Chavale's cunt. With the girl's folds

shaven, Doneshia could get right to what she wanted. She licked furiously at Chavale as Chavale opened her legs wide, struggling with the clothesline.

"Oooooh, mistress!" Chavale screamed.

Doneshia pulled her wet face out of Chavale's cunt and grinned. "That's right, baby, I'm your mistress!"

Her Beautiful Long Black Overcoat

Bill Noble

The Mercedes eased to the curb somewhere deep in San Francisco's industrial underbelly. The purr of its engine died away. Tatters of newspaper hopped and skidded under the glare of a single sputtering streetlamp.

I nervously raised an eyebrow. "Where's the club?"

"At the end of the block. Most people park around the corner on Folsom."

The "club" was the City's reigning BDSM establishment, the Cathedral. The Mercedes' diminutive driver was Caryl Leverett, sixty-something venture capitalist and one of California's most relentless Republican fundraisers (I'm a penniless liberal; at my lover's request, I'd left my Dean button in the dresser drawer). The flickering streetlight transformed Caryl's snowy hair into an improbably cherubic halo.

My lover sat quietly in the backseat, not speaking unless spoken to. I ached to touch her, to reassure or to be reassured.

Caryl cleared his throat. "Deirdre," he said. I heard the rustle as she came to attention.

"You may have forgotten about opening our doors," Caryl said. His voice held a carefully modulated mix of annoyance and indulgence.

Deirdre got out of the car, her overcoat wrapped around her just a little too tightly. She opened Caryl's door first, of course, and stepped back respectfully as he emerged; then she came and held my door. I tried to use my best puppy eyes to send a little love, but she kept her gaze obediently on the pavement. Maybe it was *me* who needed the reassurance.

Caryl handed her the keys. She opened the trunk and extracted a heavy leather duffel bag, looped its strap over her shoulder, and brought the keys back.

He smiled at me, an expansive smile for such a spit of a man—he barely cleared five-four—and lifted a black-gloved hand in the direction of the club. "Shall we go?"

As we started out, Deirdre, lugging the forty-pound bag of toys that Caryl would use on her tonight, walked a respectful half-dozen paces behind us. Had anyone been on the street to see us, we would have made a curious chiaroscuro: Caryl with his flaring eyebrows and mobile, alert face; me, a thirty-three-year-old wannabe and showing it, shivering in my just-bought black shirt and dangling triskelion from eBay; and Deirdre, elegant and silent in her ankle-length black overcoat. Her shining hair, pale in the glare of the single sodium streetlight, swept almost to her waist.

I don't know what I'd been expecting, but it wasn't a rusting, corrugated iron wall three stories high, interrupted only by an ancient door that screeched in protest as Deirdre opened it for us. And it wasn't the paunchy, broad-shouldered man in leathers who checked Caryl against the guest list and eyed my ID. And it certainly wasn't the cocktail-party decorum in the vast, complicated dungeon inside.

At the cloakroom, Deirdre shrugged quickly out of her overcoat, turning heads as she did so. Caryl's elegant leather collar emphasized the slenderness of her neck. My lithe lover—Caryl's chattel for the evening, I reminded myself—wore a black halter with bright, dangling chains that teased her nipples to perpetual arousal. Black net stockings began at mid-thigh and terminated within spike heels. The heels gleamed the color of old blood. Tension constricted my throat, but a steady clutch of arousal churned in my groin.

Caryl took me on a tour as Deirdre went, eyes down, to fetch us drinks. It was still on the early side for a San Francisco party, so only a single scene was in progress: a tall black woman systematically flogged a sinewy man who was bound over something that looked like a vaulting horse. Clusters of people chatted among the machinery, the cages, and the Saint Andrew's crosses, some in fetish gear, some in casual dress. Some of the machinery was ominously intimidating, and some of the people might have been flown in from the set of *Rocky Horror*, but what struck me most was the essential ordinariness of the low chatter.

Caryl ensconced us in high-backed chairs that faced two massive wooden crosses. When Deirdre returned, drinks in hand, he instructed her to lay out the toys. When she was through, he turned to me. "Are you still comfortable with being an observer?"

I nodded, trying a little too hard, I think, to communicate suave confidence. Maybe this evening had been a really bad idea; maybe I *didn't* want to see what my lover did on her nights out.

The ruby studs on Caryl's black shirtfront glittered. "Don't get close unless I tell you to—I don't want to worry about striking you accidentally—and as the evening gets busier, be careful not to impinge on the scenes around us. And if our play distresses you and you need to leave, no one will be offended."

He stood and led Deirdre to the right-hand cross. He

stripped her naked wordlessly; with a tightening in my stomach, I watched the first signs of heavy-lidded arousal invade her face, watched my lover give herself up utterly to this wealthy, politically alien man I'd only met once before. With an easy expertise diminished only by his straining on tiptoes to reach the high rings, he buckled her face-in, arms angled above her head, legs spread and chained at the ankles.

He flogged her. Flogged her with a skilled, relentless rhythm. Flogged her until her ass and back glowed cherry red.

The flogging was almost more than I could bear. My cock was ready to burst—and I wanted to run, to call a cab and flee for home. I was wracked with guilt for being so turned on.

He turned her face-out. I could see she was deep in what she had told me was her "sub-space," lost in the torrent of sensation and turn-on. Watching her slack face, her vulnerable breasts, her delicate genital hair—arousal and dread soared together in me.

He began flogging her again in this new position. What I had been witnessing was just the beginning. He progressed to cruel-looking, vibrating nipple clamps that pulled from her the first cries of pain and then a writhing, red-faced orgasm. A black box among the array of toys was an "electrostimulation device," something brand-new in my experience. Deirdre loosed startled howls as he probed her nipples and her now-glistening labia.

The intensity grew and grew. And my tension grew right along with it. Deirdre got together with Caryl only a few times a year, and always for power play. I knew about their relationship from the first, of course: we have no secrets from each other. I'd asked nearly a year before if I could accompany them to a scene. Power play was part of an erotic world I knew next to nothing about, but on the nights my lover disappeared into Caryl's world, I ached to know what was happening. Caryl's invitation to me had been tendered a few weeks before.

The evening had begun with dinner at a busy, fashionable restaurant. Caryl and Deirdre hadn't "played" as we ate; it was simply a social occasion. Except that Deirdre never took off the long black coat...and I never lost my awareness of what she wore—or didn't wear—beneath it, or what was happening to her nipples as she spooned her vichyssoise.

The *snap* of Caryl pulling on a latex glove brought me back into the room. Nose to nose with her, three fingers thrusting into her, he brought my lover to a pleading, head-tossing orgasm that left her hanging slack in her chains, spent. He kissed her in the aftermath, formally but quite tenderly. It wasn't a bad performance for a Republican, and it was an opportunity for me to struggle with the uncomfortable truth that their kiss churned up more jealousy than her orgasm.

He turned to me with impeccable timing: "Would you like to have a little time to connect with her?"

I mumbled something that was intended as a yes and stood. Caryl lifted Deirdre's silken hair from her face and caressed her cheek with a finger. He spoke to her gently: "Is it all right if I'm away for a few minutes?" He gestured: "He'll be here for you."

She kissed his hand in assent.

As Caryl walked away Deirdre struggled to raise her head. She brought her eyes to focus with a loving look. "Are you all right?" she murmured.

"Am *I* alright? I'm not being beaten and electrocuted!"

I stepped toward her where she hung and gave her an open-mouthed kiss. "It's hard watching. Harder than I thought."

She nudged my cock with her knee and grinned an exhausted, walleyed grin. "Good," she said, "as long as it's not *too* hard."

I brushed my lips down her neck, struggling to suppress the

fine shaking that had seized me since the flogging began. "Are *you* all right?" I asked. "And how is it having me here?"

"It's what I wanted."

Her whisper was barely audible over the tumult of the couple next to us. There, a bristly-bearded young man was flogging a porcelain-featured Chinese woman: a relentless, two-handed rain of blows, the *whack* of leather and the woman's cries almost continuous. Sweat streamed from both their bodies. Astonishingly, the woman was unrestrained: she held her body to the cross through sheer will.

Caryl returned. He gave Deirdre a drink of water and without a word, turned her so that her backside was again exposed. As he clipped in the last chains, he invited me to stand in the narrow space behind the cross. Stomach leaden with dread, I took my place.

He began again, this time wielding a flogger with a thick, braided handle and terrifyingly thin, cruel falls. My face was a foot from Deirdre's. She held my eyes with her own, wide, undefended, and blue. I shook. She was calm, transparent to the sensations that assaulted her.

This flogging made what had gone before seem like a trivial preliminary. Caryl had unbuttoned his shirt and rolled up his sleeves. His hair whipped his face as he whipped my lover. My nostrils filled with the stench of leather and pain. As the session intensified, my ears filled with my lover's cries, wrenched from her, impact after impact.

But from so intimate a distance, I saw something I hadn't seen before: this fed her. I was watching a religious ritual. My lover reached through the pain to something beyond her, something lovemaking alone couldn't take her to. My arousal remained, painful and unresolved, but my anguish receded. My shaking nearly ceased.

Caryl's blows doubled in intensity. His pace quickened. I grasped the wooden beams of the cross and let the concussions flow into my own body. *I understood. I finally understood!*

How long they went on, I couldn't say. A long time. Deirdre's cries grew louder and wilder, her voice breaking, her breath coming in desperate gulps. But she never pled for mercy, never asked Caryl to back off. She took as much as he could give.

Finally he was done. Or she was. I couldn't name the thing that had been communicated between them as she stood, spread-eagled in chains, eyes fixed on mine.

He took her down with delicate gentleness, and I discovered that I had reentered my body enough to make a joke, even if I did it silently. *I've finally figured out what the fuck a compassionate conservative is!* Deirdre folded herself into his arms—collapsed, really—and he held her. He turned her face to his and kissed her, a profound, long-continued kiss. I'm not sure I've ever seen someone kiss so tenderly.

I brought them a large cup of water and he gave her sip after sip, his face close, breathing with her. And then he laid her gently on the floor. He spread her long black coat over her and knelt with his hands resting on her body for several long minutes.

"Come and sit here," he said, offering me his place. He withdrew to the chairs.

I sat, holding her, listening to the thud of my heart.

Finally she stirred, ready to rouse. He motioned me aside.

She looked up as he stooped and snapped a leash onto her collar. This was another transition, I saw. The purely physical domination was over; I knew from our talk in the car that he was about to parade her naked and in near-trance through the club. She was now his slave, to be displayed for something much more public than the flogging. In his narrow gray eyes, I saw the first uncurtained emotion he had betrayed all evening: lust. His lust to own this beautiful, naked, defenseless woman

He gave a sharp tug on the leash...and she stuck her tongue out at him, her pink, impudent tongue.

Not just a little way out. Not my lover. No, this was a full-blown, in your face, definitely Democratic *fuck you if you think I'm that easy!*

It surprised him. I saw his split second of indecision.

And then I saw the Bush Pioneer swing into action, the million-dollar fundraiser, the white-maned, five-foot-four eminence of kinky Silicon Valley megabucks. That tiny white-haired man grabbed my five-foot-six, hundred-and-thirty-pound naked lover—and upended her. Jesse Ventura couldn't have done it better.

She shrieked.

She was over his knee. She flailed, but he had her, helpless.

His hand went up.

It landed with a *smack!* that turned every eye in the club. Over the background noise of whipping and flogging, over the groans of the inflicted and the grunts of the inflictors, the intent of that sound was unmistakable.

"Caryl!" she screamed. *Smack!*

"Whatthefuckdoyou..." *Smack!*

Smack!

Smack!

"Noooooooooooo!" I'd never heard Deirdre wail.

Smack! Smack! Smack! The pace never varied. He never lost his grip through all her frenzied thrashings, never lost his look of privileged determination.

Her butt was already red from flogging; now it flamed. I could see every handprint, one layered atop another. *Smack! Smack! Smack! Smack! Smack!*

She went slack in surrender, then roused again. "You sonofabitch!" She bellowed this at the top of her lungs. If anybody had been lurking in the shadows on Folsom Street at that hour, he would have heard her.

Smack! Smack! Smack!

With every smack my cock cranked another notch toward vertical. With every smack, I didn't think it was possible to get any harder—but I did. The glands in my jaw cramped. I ground my teeth.

She was clawing his shirt, trying to rip his six-hundred-dollar pants to shreds. If his balls had been in reach, she would have torn them off. No luck. *Smack! Smack! Smack!* He wasn't going to stop. Not while an atom of resistance remained in her.

Smack! Smack! Smack! I was laughing. I was crying.

Deirdre's no wimp. It took a long time.

I let the two of them sit up front on the long drive home. Deirdre leaned her head on his shoulder and reached back between the seats to twine her fingers with mine.

Caryl shook my hand on the front steps, the perfect right-wing gentleman. If he noticed the cock jutting in the front of my pants or the big red, white, and blue Dean placard on our door, he never said a word. He kissed Deirdre with melting sweetness, his fingers slipping into the belt of the black overcoat to pull her close. And then he was gone.

It was late enough it was almost early. We snapped off the light and tumbled into bed, Deirdre's beautiful long black overcoat abandoned on the floor, its arms flung out in surrender. When I closed my eyes, I imagined it swirling upright next to the bed to stand guard over us.

We lay immobile for perhaps five minutes, blankly surprised we were still conscious.

"Well, shit," I said.

"Me neither," she sighed. "Too turned on."

I turned on the bedside lamp. "I gotta fuck you."

The overcoat had no response to that, but Deirdre did: "You better."

She heaved herself up and crouched at the edge of the mattress. I crawled out of bed to stand behind her. The whole evening had been foreplay: she reached around and slid me right in.

We fucked. I jerked her hips and thrust. She bunted her ass against me with each stroke, giving as good as she got. I thought I heard her mutter.

"What?"

"I didn't say anything," she said. "I thought *you* did. Jesus, my ass is hypersensitive." Even in the low light it glowed, patterned with handprints.

What could I do? I brought my arm back...farther back... all the way back...and came down on that beautiful, well-used ass with all my might. *Smack!*

"Aaaaaaaaaa," she said, and clamped my cock. I thrust so hard my balls were going to be bruised in the morning.

Smack!

"Harder," she gasped.

"Slap you harder?"

"Asshole. *Fuck* me harder."

What the hell. I did. She howled. *Smack!*

"More!" She twisted her head just enough to stick out her tongue at me. *Smack!*

Three triumphant but slightly cockeyed Howard Deans smiled their approval from postcards stuck around the dresser mirror. The overcoat tangled itself around my ankles. A come was on its way through my body that was going to rip my whole pelvis wide open. Hers too.

Smack!

Smack!

Smack!

Zip Me, Hug Me, Fill My Life with Meaning

Joy James

You know the feeling. Or is it just me? Don't all women long to be zipped up? Preferably by the hands of another.

"Oh, honey, would you terribly mind zipping me up," you say, though you're perfectly capable of doing it yourself. After all, you will have, in the course of a lifetime, done it thousands of times: reaching both hands behind your waist till they find the small of your back, pressing one hand on the fabric tight against the skin where the curve of your butt begins, while the thumb and forefinger of your other hand grasps the zipper. Up you go until you can't reach any further, usually where the back of your bra is hooked. Then from the front you stretch both arms, bending at the elbows, over your shoulders for the final tug.

It sounds so funny, sort of exotic, erotic even, when you put it into words. Like watching yourself in the mirror. I've never really thought about zipping up quite that way before. Like all women, I just do it. Second nature. Still, it's *not* natural—these contortions. But neither is the best sex, come to think of it. So when my boyfriend of the moment, Victor—sweet

Victor—buys me a skintight catsuit and wants to zip me up in it, I don't demur. Besides the zipper up the back, it has one in the crotch. Victor insists on my letting him zip shut both.

Sweet, sexy—and insecure—Victor. He's a writer (isn't everyone nowadays?), but unlike most (the bloggers and such), he's trying to make a living at it. He says it doesn't bother him that I make lots more money than he does. But he always asks if it bothers me. Quite frankly, it only bothers me when he keeps bringing it up, seeking reassurance. I've got enough problems at work—where I've carefully built a reputation as a hotshot corporate litigator in the city's most prestigious law firm—without having to worry about Victor's fragile male ego at home. I simply try to avoid his seeing me in one of my countless professionally tailored—but still short-skirted—business suits.

Now naked but not. That's how I feel walking—or is it more like gliding, dancing?—around the cozy apartment this lazy Saturday morning. When I go outside, I dress the unitard up with a Hermes scarf around the waist. Wherever I go, whatever I do—even the most mundane chores—Victor's eyes follow me. Sweet Victor, he can't get enough.

When he finally pulls me to him for a long, deep kiss, I don't feel his tongue or lips so much as his strong yet always sensitive hands. They slide along my second-skinned, spandex-encased body. They stroke and caress all the curves that make me, shape me into, a woman. My curves somehow seem more contoured, more enhanced, more femininely alluring, while the things I hate about my body seem hidden, or at least subdued. It's as if the catsuit is my plastic surgeon, and I've never felt so sexy. Certainly, Victor has never found me so desirable. A woman knows.

I know that in just a moment his hands will slip behind me to pull the zipper down, slide me out of the spandex, lay me down on the sofa, and fuck me. But I'm wrong. Instead, he lifts me into his arms and carries me to the kitchen table. I hear the clanging and crashing of our breakfast dishes as Victor sweeps his hands across the table to make room for my new body. He spreads my legs that are dangling over the table's edge, and yanks down the zipper of the catsuit crotch. My cunt must be wet and welcoming, for it takes just one powerful thrust and he's in, all the way in, as deep as he's ever been inside me.

And just as quickly, it seems, he is out. It happens so fast that I can't believe it. He comes, comes so hard I imagine it shooting so far up inside me I can taste it with my tongue. I come too, simultaneously.

Tightness: that's the sensation, I want it to linger. His swollen cock inside, the spandex enclosing me outside. His cock may become limp, but I can be tight in the spandex forever. Clearly, Victor doesn't want me to take it off either. Ever. He zips me back up, as if to keep his wetness from dripping out of me. Some gets on his fingers, which he then brushes against my lips. I lick. Yes, now I can really taste it. It's so white and pure, in contrast to the catsuit's midnight blackness.

"You're my little slut," he whispers. He's never called me that before. Curiously, I like it. So I nod and say, "Yes, I'm your slut." I smile. Then, laughing, I say, "I want more, please."

"Your wish is my command." He pauses. "But first I have a little surprise for you."

"You're full of surprises today, aren't you?"

He says nothing, only smiles mysteriously, then disappears out of the room. I feel wonderfully limp, can hardly move, but manage somehow to climb down from the kitchen table. I wander into the living room, catch sight of myself in the mirror, and like what I see. I rub my hands up and down the tight spandex, and like what I feel. Only my hands, I realize—plus my face and blonde, shoulder-length hair—are not part of the rest of my body, the blackness, the tightness. In such stark contrast, just like Victor's cum.

It's at times like this that I can't help but ponder the meaning of life. The sensations turn into abstractions. Victor is an exploding star, and I, insatiable, a collapsing black hole. Energy. It's all about energy, masculine and feminine energy, and sex is the way we humans express it. The tighter the blackness enveloping me, the more I crave to be filled.

Victor will never feel what I feel, of course. But he must understand—with that ever-so-masculine, endlessly calculating, creative mind of his—for he suddenly reappears with a pile of what I can only surmise is bondage gear stacked in his arms. Clearly, the catsuit was just some kind of test, and I passed.

He spreads the gear on the living room floor. I settle myself down in the midst of it, as does Victor. We're like two children playing, sitting cross-legged, our knees touching, giggling and laughing as we discover a treasure chest of brand-new toys.

"And what's this little thingie?" I dangle a latex strap with a little rubber ball.

"It's called a ball gag, I think," Victor enlightens me. "I tighten it around your head, and the ball fits in your mouth."

"Like stretching my lips around your cock." I giggle.

"Exactly." Victor laughs. "But this hard rubber ball will never get soft."

"And this? And this?" I keep asking, as my fingers play with each item. For some of the things even Victor doesn't know their precise name, or at least he feigns ignorance. Or perhaps they are ultimately unknowable, like the cosmos itself. I want to know.

Soon I find myself stripping off the spandex catsuit and pouring my body into its black latex replacement. Victor helps tug in all the strategic places. For the final touch, of course, he zips it up. But there are not just the single zippers up the back and in the crotch. A separate zipper runs up my ass, and the metal teeth around my neck apparently zip to the matching hood that Victor now holds in his hands.

I take one final look at myself before Victor slides the hood over my head. I like what I see. If I were a guy, yes, I couldn't wait to fuck me. So fuckable: I wonder why exactly. I ask Victor.

"Can't put it into words," he says.

"Have you ever done this before? I mean, with another woman?"

"You're the first." I don't know whether to believe him.

"But it must be a fantasy you've always had, right?" I say. "You didn't just now suddenly come up with the idea? Or is it something about me that needs to be suited up, constricted like this?" I giggle again, a tad nervously, as he slips the hood over my head. I keep talking—babbling, Victor would call it. Clearly he has not the slightest interest in dialogue at this point, intent as he is on zipping the hood properly in place.

"It's an interesting fetish, I've got to admit." My words are a bit garbled now, with the press of the latex around my mouth. "I've seen pictures and stuff, but never imagined myself actually doing it, you know?" He doesn't respond. "Victor, say something, talk to me."

"You're not supposed to talk," he says in a stern voice I've never heard before. "Your mouth is not for talking. It's for taking cock."

"But..." Whatever it is I'm about to say is cut off by the ball gag Victor sticks in my mouth. I can see him now in the mirror tightening the strap behind my head.

It's the last thing I see, for suddenly Victor snaps two little flaps attached to the hood over my eyes. Reflexively my hands move to my face, but Victor grabs them and pulls them behind my back, where I can feel him tying them tightly together. Ever so tightly, with one of those long rubber cords

I glimpsed just moments ago among all the bondage gear.

"How's that, my little slut?" Victor whispers so softly I can hardly hear him—or maybe it's just the hood over my ears? It's a rhetorical question, I know. Still, I try to answer, to say something. But all that comes out of my mouth is a whimpering squeal.

"Remember, no sounds! Your mouth is a just a hole to receive my cock, anytime at my will." And he tightens the ball gag even more. I can't help but emit some sound, any sound: it comes out no more than a gurgle. If my colleagues at the law office could hear—and see!—me now. Never afraid to aggressively voice my opinion, I was even once called an "uppity bitch" by an angry male partner. Now I finally "know my place," he would no doubt say. I have to laugh. But it's not laughter I hear, just some kind of noise. So Victor tightens the gag still more.

Then I feel a tightening sensation around my waist. This must be the rubber corset, one of the first pieces of bondage gear I had noticed and fingered when Victor presented his collection. The waist was so tiny I wondered how in the world I would ever fit in that part of Victor's fantasy. His vigorous tugging on the cords in the eyelets now tells me how. My body twists and quivers as he shapes me to his desire.

The wiggling embodiment of male fantasy, all boobs and bottom and wet-lipped receptivity, that's what I've become. With my body bound, my identity reduced to a wasp-waisted shape, I exist only in Victor's perceptions. Blindfolded, all that I can see is what my mind's eye visualizes; that is, what I imagine Victor must see. As if in a sensory deprivation chamber, I have no interaction with the outside world: no mouth to talk, no free hands to gesture. Without the distractions of outside stimuli, I can luxuriate in just being an empty space to be filled with desire. Any perception is limited to hood-muffled hearing, the smell and taste of a rubber gag, and touch, of course—the exquisite sense of being tightly, ever so tightly, hugged all over.

Yes, hug me, please. Tighter. That's what I want. That's what Victor wants. I have become him, the one who perceives me, with all his senses. Me, an object, a sex object, no more, no less. I desire what he desires. His desire creates me.

Fill me up. Make me full. Fullness, tightness, that's what I need. The tighter the latex, the more constricted my body, the more I need to be filled. All my energy is bound into the hole that I now am, a collapsing sun, a cosmic black hole, wanting to suck everything in. Nature abhors a vacuum.

Victor sticks what must be a dildo, so thick and so long, in my cunt. Then he zips up the latex crotch to hold it in place. Next he forces a butt plug into my bottom, and zips that up, too. But he knows that I am not yet completely full, so he pushes me to the floor, kneeling. He removes the ball gag from my mouth and then inserts his cock, as firm as I've ever felt it, deep down my throat.

Full, so full, full at last. I never knew how full I could feel. Full of meaning, even. My seemingly successful workaday life seems nothing but emptiness now. I'm no longer a lawyer but a cumhole, therefore I am.

"You slut!" Victor groans. I can feel, but can not taste, the release as he shoots straight down my throat.

Now soft and slippery, his cock slides out of my mouth. I can speak again. And this is what I say: "Honey, will you zip me up please?"

Mahia's Truth

M. Christian

Much has been said, and no doubt will continue to be said, about Subadar Mahia—yet much is not honestly known about him. If anyone, even today, were to ask Constable Sutia about him, he would have to shrug his old shoulders and admit to knowing little save Mahia's title, only that the Subadar had an older sister who lived in town, and that people said that he was brilliant. Others, more in tune with Mahia's presence, could add a little more: that he was unmarried, that he was educated far beyond even his lofty title, that he moved in a way that when at first beheld seemed to make little or no sense but when his actions (such as those involving a criminal investigation) had concluded you could see that how he had accomplished his goal was straight and true as an arrow—but one launched from a completely unexpected direction.

It was best, these people said, to simply allow him his way and let him work his magic.

But when the Subadar said to Constable Sutia that day in the Surimia jail, "Please leave me with him for a moment. An hour or two will be best," the reason the elder constable did so wasn't so much as from respect or a knowledge of Mahia's working practices as it was just from an eagerness to return to his midday nap.

Alone with him, the Subadar took the prisoner in with a few precise swipes of his incredibly focused eyes.

The man was young, probably near to twenty-six years of age. His hair was brown, but of a shade not common to the region. His body was strong and lean, not overly muscular. His face, what the Subadar could see of it, was angled almost like a Yankee and not like any other ethnic type he could immediately perceive. The man's dress didn't bear out the Constable's initial assessment of a "man with little or no means": while he was dressed simply, the clothes were only slightly worn out in places. The man, obviously, had access to some funds—if only enough to keep food in his belly and clothes on his back.

"There was a reported theft in the marketplace. An item of jewelry was reported stolen from the establishment of Ling Po. As the constables of the town questioned those in the area you attempted to flee. When told to halt, you redoubled your stride. Innocence or guilt I cannot determine instantly, sir, but I can say that your actions spoke of a man not wishing to be questioned, or inquired of. Will you, this instant, say why you attempted to flee Constable Sutia's deputies?"

The man's only response to Mahia's eloquent description of the incident in the marketplace that day was to lift his head for a moment, as if to study the Subadar in the poor jail light.

What the prisoner saw was a tall, thin reed of a man. Skin the color of polished, aged coal. A regal, infinitely patient face slow to move, revealing nothing of the soul beneath. Eyes that played and danced with a kind of laughing at the world they saw. His features were light and crisp, as if he were made of stone polished to a near transparency. The Subadar was dressed in a simple suit, very formal for the small town—but it wasn't a pompous suit worn to impress the simple townspeople. Rather, it was part of the man. Looking at him it was hard to see Mahia without his white suit, it was as much him as were the bones of his elegant face.

His voice, police brethren said, was a blackjack dipped in honey.

"The truth, it seems, needs to be revealed. But that is a word that has confounded some of the greatest minds through the history of mankind. It is a quick word, a word that can hide anywhere for anyone. So many kinds, as well. My truth. Your truth. Everyone's different, you see, yet each describes the same world, at the same moment. But we are not here for me to discourse on philosophy. I am here as a Subadar of the Northern Providences, and I ask you in that official capacity the question your attempt to escape and subsequent silence has forced me to ask: did you take an item of jewelry from Ling Po's emporium?"

The accused looked up upon being spoken to, his eyes locking with Mahia's. As the Subadar finished, the man spoke: "I did not, sir."

"Ah, at least we have established communication. Why then, if you are innocent of the crime the deputies were investigating, did you run?"

At this the man simply shook his head and again looked at the ground.

"Your refusal to answer puzzles me. You do not explain. You do not protest. You do not offer to even have your pockets turned out to prove that you do not have the item."

"The deputies searched me."

"Ah. Further speech from you. Good! But you see even the volunteering of this information would be a sign that you wish to be considered innocent. But this near silence begs that you hide something—and when one is accused of a crime, sir, that is what you must not do."

The Subadar studied the man a moment, scanning him from simple shoes to the black hair on his finely formed head. He watched his eyes and the lines of his mouth. The man had a pleasing face, one that Mahia could easily see smiling or laughing despite his current dour mask. "I see I am forced to take an angle with this interview that I would not normally take. I admit to you a fault, sir, in that I am pressed for time in this matter: my sister plans to be wed and since I am the eldest of the family it is my duty to inspect her choice in husbands. He is due to arrive tonight on the 6:15 train and I must not be late and, thus, not accomplish my familiar duties. Stand and take off your pants."

The man's face went blank for a second. It was as if his muscles had let go of their moorings with shock and confusion. So confused was he by this odd, if not normally rude, request, that he actually started to stand.

"Yes, sir, you heard me right. The request for you to remove your trousers was a sincere and correct one. Please do so and I will explain."

The man stood all the way up and hesitated as the Subadar reached into the interior pocket of his simple suit and produced a black shoestring, saying, "There are indeed many, many forms of truth. All faiths teach their own particular view, as do even those who claim no divine powers have any sway in their lives. The government speaks one, family speaks another. You speak yours, I speak mine. Often, though, the truth that wins in all these matters is the one that simply speaks it the loudest. It is not a proud fact, but in the history of us all it is one, nevertheless. I am here as Subadar of the Northern Province to ascertain if you should be formally arrested and charged with the crime of theft, or released back into the world. I am here to find out my truth in this."

The man, meanwhile, had stood, kicked off his shoes and, as requested by the dark and elegant Mahia, removed his simple trousers. His legs were strong, long, and rippled with muscles from walking or running. The skin on his legs was as tan as that on his face, and hazy with a slight dust of curly hairs. The man's sex was uncut and large, lying in a field of those hairs like a small reddish urn. His testicles were all but invisible behind it.

The Subadar of the Northern Province was silent for a moment, then he spoke and instructed. "Excellent. Now sit down on the bunk and spread your legs apart."

As instructed, the accused did so—the bed creaking and groaning in protest.

Mahia took his regular black shoestring and performed some kind of quick sleight-of-hand magic on it, transforming its humble length into a baroque series of knots and loops—then, with more deft handwork, he calmly and quickly, almost as if transformed into a doctor performing a regulation examination, lifted the man's large testicles and deftly inserted them and the man's penis into the loops and knots. When he was finished, in what must have been nothing but a handful of seconds, he had the man's testicles and penis neatly bundled in the cord with a longer length trailing up and into the Subadar's hand.

"A technique," he explained, pulling once, sharply, on the cord, "taught to me by a fellow police officer a long time ago. The principle is almost too obvious to explain but I feel I must at least calm your fears: there is no pain involved in what you could call 'Mahia's truth.' I will not harm you or cause you any immediate pain. I will however, because it is my duty as a Subadar, discover the truth of this situation. Now, I ask you again, did you take the jewelry?"

The man said, simply, shortly, "I did not."

"Why did you run from the officers?"

When the man did not respond, Mahia jerked the cord, sharply, causing the pan's penis to slap up hard against his shirt and belly. In the simple cell it was like a hand slap. The man responded with an eye-widening stare and a quick intake of breath. All but instantly, his penis began to grow stiff and large, eventually almost straining against the cord binding it.

Again Mahia jerked the cord and again the man's eyes widened—but this time a sharp hiss escaped his lips and he leaned back against the cracked and peeling plaster wall, his back stiffening in what appeared to be extreme pleasure.

"I'm sure if you've taken the ring you'd realize it. Quite a lovely ring, or so I've been informed: a gold setting, like three ropes coiled around one another. Two pearls and one medium-sized sapphire. Have you seen it?"

The man shook his head and, once again, Mahia jerked the cord. The man moaned in response, moving his hands toward the cords binding his testicles and penis. The actions, though, were not ones of pain—rather, one could easily deduce from the great size of his penis (easily eight, perhaps nine inches) that he was more than enjoying the binding of it, thus he was reaching not to remove the lace but rather to stimulate himself further.

Subadar Mahia slapped him, once. In the small cell the sound was sharp and quick, more an explosion of sound than one of violence. Shocked, the man fell back with a heavy thud against the wall of the cell and looked up at the calm and refined Mahia with eyes grown large with excitement and, maybe, fear.

"I do apologize, but it is integral to this operation, you see, that you keep your hands on the bed and away from yourself. If you do so again I will have to stop completely, and thus end this line of questioning."

The man thought for a moment, then nodded. "I apologize," he said, making himself more comfortable on the cot by moving himself back from the edge of it and putting his back flat against the wall.

"Thank you. I ask you again. Did you take the ring? It was not found on you when you were searched so you either dropped it off somewhere—where it could be retrieved later, no doubt—or passed it along to a confederate in the marketplace. Please speak the truth."

The accused man's penis looked for all the world like it wished more than anything to leap from his hairy lap with its exalted pleasure at this treatment by the Subadar: it was incredibly large and pulsed with a heartbeat rhythm, bobbing up and down, up and down—almost to his legs and almost to his shirt. At the end of it, a small dot of white jism grew and slowly started to run down from the hidden tip past the swollen head. The man's groans were almost as rhythmic as the bobbing of his penis—with each jerk of the cord, he grunted and moaned in near ecstasy, his hands digging into the thin sheets and mattress of the cot to keep himself from crying out in pleasure.

"Why did you run from the officers? Why did you flee?"

The man took his hands from the mattress and moved them quickly, almost a blur, to his penis. Instantly Mahia stopped his jerking of the cord and moved as if to remove it before the man could stroke his throbbing penis. But rather than grab it and end the "line of questioning" the man grabbed the iron of his knotted thighs instead and dug his strong hands in so hard that Mahia was surprised he didn't start to bleed from the pressure.

"Why did you flee? Did you take the ring? Answer me, please, sir. Answer me or I will stop this right now!"

The man started to whip his head back and forth, a perpendicular metronome to the jerking and pulsing of his penis, shaking his head that either he wouldn't answer or that he didn't want Mahia to stop. In his throws of throbbing pleasure, he had started to bite and chew his lip. His eyes were closed some of the time but when they were open Mahia could see that they were dilated into two brown pools of vibrating pleasure, like dark tea set on a long, low boil.

Mahia changed the tune of his jerking on the cord, now using slow hard jerks as opposed to his previous fluttering twitches with it. The man actually screamed a lion's roar of frustration and sexual pleasure and dug even harder into his own thighs to keep himself from touching his now almost purple and swollen manhood.

Suddenly, the Subadar stopped his movement of the man's penis altogether. A heavy, painful silence filled the room. "Answer me now. *Answer me now*," Mahia said.

The man started to quickly mutter something, but his words were too soft for Mahia to hear easily. "Whisper," he told the man in gentle tones, "in my ear."

With tears of pain, frustration and pleasure the man whispered something into the ear of Subadar Mahia. Whatever it was he said, he had all but no effect on the polished ebony of the Subadar's face. Mahia simply listened to the man's words, calmly jerking the cord tied around the man's penis and testicles once or twice to keep the flow of confession coming.

When the man was finished, he leaned back, sobbing deep and hard in his chest, hands still gripping like vices on his bruised thighs.

Without a word, the Subadar of the Northern Province put his hand on the man's penis and stroked him once, slowly—using the man's leaking jism as a form of lubricant. One stroke, two—Mahia's hands were as gentle as his soul, as smooth as his demeanor. Faster, faster he stroked till the man gave an animal scream of pure joy, jetting his seed out into the cool air of the cell to fall on the rough boards between his feet.

Mahia took a plain white handkerchief and dotted the perspiration off the now panting, almost crying, man's forehead and then cleaned off his seed from his lap and his own hands.

"You are free to go," Mahia told him, leaving the door to the cell open as he stepped out.

Mahia found Constable Sutia basking in the fading late-afternoon light, calmly working his way through a giant bowl of ripe figs. Surprised, Sutia sprang comically to his feet and wiped his sticky fingers on his wrinkled and ill-fitting uniform. "Subadar!" he exclaimed. "Did you get the man to confess?"

"I am sorry for your deputies, Constable," Mahia said, folding his handkerchief neatly and putting it in his pocket, "for it seems they will need to continue their investigations: the man, it is very clear to me—beyond a doubt—is innocent."

"But Subadar, he ran when questioned!"

"He ran from nothing but a moment of guilt over his reason for being in the marketplace, Constable. He is a simple man who only sought companionship. He believed that was the crime he was being sought for."

"You are convinced of this?"

"I am, Constable."

"Then that is assurance enough for me, Subadar. That is more than enough for me."

After that, simple and hearty thanks were given from Sutia to Mahia and they began to part—with Sutia's assurance that the prisoner would be given back his belongings and given a meal to apologize for his detainment.

Before leaving, Mahia gave Sutia the address of his older sister's house, with the instructions to pass it along to the man they had suspected of the theft. "Tell him that it would be my honor to put him up for the night at my sister's to make up for any discomfort I might have caused him."

Sutia did so and Subadar Mahia went off toward town, walking into fading sunlight.

The Divan

N. T. Morley

Lady Jennifer Partridge would never have gone to her ex-lover's house if she hadn't known that he would seduce her. But seduction was the furthest thing from Gustav's mind.

It was not a sense of nostalgia or any form of obligation that brought Lady Jennifer Partridge to the mansion that night. Jenna felt that she owed him nothing; in fact, if anything, he owed her. For seventeen months the young bride-to-be had carried on a torrid affair behind her fiancée's back, only calling it quits on the night before her wedding when Gustav Braeburn, as he usually did, had tied her to the bed in his dungeon and fucked her quite soundly till she knew she would barely be able to walk down the aisle. Then, freed from his expertly-tied knots with the thing that he always used to release her—Gustav's pearl-handled switchblade, imported at great price from the continent—she had dressed somberly, shared with Gustav a postcoital brandy in the parlor, and informed him that it was over between them.

"It's all well and good to do what we've done when I'm engaged," Jenna told him. "But I intend to turn over a new leaf. From now on, I shan't return your calls."

"You'll return them," Gustav told her, lounging decadently on his favorite overstuffed armchair. "And you'll be back for more of the same. The first time you don't come when he fucks you, you'll be here as fast as you can find a taxi."

Gustav was wrong about that. In fact, it was twenty-four times on the nose that Lewis Partridge fucked his wife without making her come before she returned to her lover. She had kept count, in a little diary she kept in her night table. There, she recorded her every sexual adventure, misadventure, and fantasy—in French, a language Lewis did not speak. She wrote in secret and locked her diary with a tiny padlock. The only key rested between her breasts, tucked into a locket on a golden chain. The locket also held a picture of her husband. Through her entire courtship and into her marriage night, the locket had held a picture of Gustav—and knowing that, at any moment, Lewis might have asked to see inside it had always given Jenna an incalculable thrill. It was not until they returned from their honeymoon that Jenna had replaced the photograph with one of her husband. Gustav had seen the locket through their dalliance, and she had noticed his eyes resting on it as he'd kissed her demurely at the reception line. He knew that his photograph rested inside, but he knew nothing of the key.

Unlike the tedious nights to come, on that first night, their wedding night, all had been bliss. Jenna had indeed climaxed profoundly on her husband's cock. For more than three years, since Lewis had first invited the eighteen-year-old heiress to a party on his yacht, she had anticipated the moment of first sex with her husband—not because she found him particularly attractive, but because she knew it would cement her life in the gentry, a life of leisure as the treasured wife of a nobleman. From the first, his sexual interest in her was plain, but when it became clear—that first night, no less—that he was marriage-minded, she had resolved to delay her gratification in order to win his respect—and, she admitted only to herself, ignorance of her true nature. Their long courtship had involved nothing more than deep kisses and an occasional straying hand, always met with perfectly acted offense on Jenna's part. The one feel she gave him was two weeks before their wedding, and she ensured even that bit of innocent stroking remained above the waist. Lewis Partridge had soaked the front of his pants with one hand molded on his fiancée's left breast, and Jenna had pretended offense, a lie that Lewis believed with an urgency that astounded even Jenna. After she'd made him leave, she licked her hand, sticky with her fiancée's seed, and immediately called Gustav, who did much more to her petite breasts than merely touch them.

But when it was time, Jenna's eagerness to consummate her new contract combined with so many other factors to drive her into the heights of passion, making it difficult for her to play the part of the blushing bride. Oh, she managed, but only with great effort, forcing her hands not to roam over her new husband's body, making them rest tangled in her bridal skirts as he plumbed her depths until Lewis—quite to Jenna's surprise—suggested that he enter her from behind. She made him convince her, which he did with such tentative want that Jenna finally lost patience and put her ass in the air, abandoning her show of reluctance.

Jenna found herself intoxicated not only from the half dozen or so glasses of champagne she'd consumed, but from all the attention she'd received and, most importantly, the envelopes stuffed with money. Glorious in her lovely dress, the new Lady Jennifer Partridge had enjoyed herself quite vigorously, before she could even remove her dress and show off the lovely corset and garters—sans panties—she had worn through the entire reception, its tight embrace reminding her of the many ways in which Gustav had restrained her over their seventeen months of illicit meetings. Lewis had thrilled to find his new wife shaved—a trait Gustav had always required of her—and if he had noticed that his lovely young bride was not a virgin, he did not mention it.

She would vividly remember that first orgasm Lewis gave her, as if it were to be her last. She remembered it not only because of its intensity, but because at the moment of her climax she was bent forward, ass in the air, knees spread wide—exactly the way she had been fucked by Gustav the previous night. She was gripping the headboard with her hands, and when she looked down at her wrists she saw that the diamond bracelets she wore—wedding gifts from her husband to provide her with "something new"—had slipped forward, their clasps askew, revealing the red marks that Gustav's ropes had left on her wrists not eighteen hours before. It was that moment of pride and arousal at seeing the rope marks—and, perhaps, the thrill of knowing that at any moment Lewis might notice them, too—that drove Jenna to an unparalleled climax, one that brought the image into her mind, unbidden, of Gustav Braeburn, his face twisted in a cruel smile as he punished her bound and gagged body with his cock.

Jenna feigned virtue throughout her first weeks of marriage, thrilling at the ease with which she managed to make her first blow job, given only at Lewis's insistence, seem awkward and inexpert. In fact, Lady Jennifer was an expert cocksucker, having been trained extensively by Gustav, who liked his head deep and rough before he blessed her with a mouthful of his seed. Jenna had already been orally skilled before she ever met Lewis or Gustav, having made several trips—in complicated disguises—to the waterfront, to thrill at learning the marital trade, both before and after Lewis proposed. It was there, from rough men who took her orally one after another, that she learned what she liked and, more importantly, how much she liked and resolved to get it only when its achievement could not damage her social standing. She had done exactly that, and by the time Gustav had met her there—a wealthy man who also haunted the docks for his thrills—she was ready for him.

And now, after six months of marriage and twenty-four anorgasmic trysts with her husband, Jenna was ready for Gustav again.

"You've a new divan," said Jenna, swirling brandy around her snifter as she entered the parlor of Gustav's mansion. "Oriental, if I'm not mistaken."

"I'm afraid it's a copy, my dear," said Gustav, his lips twisting in a smile as he toyed with the tie of his silk robe. It was just like Gustav to receive her as if he were ready for bed—but not for sleep. In fact, she had expected it, and it had not caused her discomfort. After all, she had seen him naked quite often enough, so the sight of him in a robe should cause no reaction.

Jenna gave him a tight smile that was half frown, and both knew what it meant. This, along with Gustav's low social standing, was why she would never have married him, why he was fit only for the kind of illicit tryst that had satisfied her for a time, before her marriage. "You're quite right, however, it's ancient Chinese in style. It's a copy of a piece that sat in the emperor's palace, with a few modern touches. I dare say it's worth more than the original."

"I doubt that," said Jenna with an unmistakable sneer.

"Oh, it's worth very much to me," said Gustav. "Try it out."

"All right," said Jenna, seating herself on the divan. It was quite comfortable. She wore a long red dress with a rather daring slit up the middle, well past her knees. She was wearing nothing underneath, a further risk that she took in coming to Gustav's place. The knowledge of it intoxicated her. Still, it would not do to show her hand too early, and Jenna crossed her legs quite daintily as she reclined into the soft cushions.

"Hardly a decent copy," said Jenna. "I'm sure the emperor did not have polyurethane foam."

"Nor did he have titanium," said Gustav, taking a seat in his overstuffed armchair. "But we'll discuss that later. Get comfortable, Lady Partridge. You've been comfortable here many times before, haven't you? Take off your shoes."

The suggestion was given almost like a command, and Jenna's instincts took over. She obeyed, kicking off her high-heeled pumps and relaxing into the divan. She reddened as she realized the ease with which she'd followed Gustav's suggestion—but if he had planned to tease her about it, he thought better. Instead, he spoke softly to her, the rumble of his voice as seductive as she remembered it from the first time it had graced her ears, from far above her as she knelt on the docks, his sailor's pants opened and his cock in her mouth. "So, Jen, I hear the esteemed Lord Partridge is on a business trip in Germany. When the cat's away, the mouse will play?"

"I'm known as Lady Jennifer, now, and you'd do well to remember it." This was not strictly true; Lewis, her friends, and her family still called her "Jenna"—and only Gustav had ever called her "Jen." "And," she continued, "I'm hardly here to play. *You* called me, remember? What was so important that you simply *had* to discuss it with me?" She laughed, derisive. "You can't be pregnant."

"Nor can you," said Gustav. "I understand he barely fucks you."

"There's more to marriage than fucking," said Jenna. "But then, I wouldn't expect you to know that. Besides, Lewis fucks me just fine. He's quite a tender lover. You wouldn't understand that, either."

"No," said Gustav. "I wouldn't. And that's why you agreed to see me, isn't it?"

Jenna felt her pulse pounding, the heat starting in earnest between her thighs. She had shaved in anticipation of this meeting, and every movement she made drew her freshly shorn lips against each other, sending a tingle through her body. She had been wet since the moment she'd shimmied into her slinky dress, a dress she had never worn for Lewis—what would be the point? But now the hunger started in earnest, and she could feel her clitoris swelling in a way it hadn't since her first night with Lewis, the tiny bud's fullness nestled snugly between the smooth lips of her sex.

"Not at all. I agreed to see you out of pity. You seem quite hung up on me. You haven't accepted that I'm married."

"Oh, I've accepted it," said Gustav. "If anything, it makes you more desirable. And if there's any pity to be had, it belongs to you, my dear."

"You're as callous as you are arrogant," said Jenna, the growing hardness of her nipples bringing a hint of discomfort as they began to show through the thin fabric of her dress.

"How's your drink?" smiled Gustav. "Ready for a refill?"

"Almost," she said, swirling the remaining finger of brandy as her hand rested on the divan's comfortable arm.

"Good," said Gustav, and it all happened at once.

Had she been watching her ex-lover more closely, Jenna Partridge would have seen his hand creeping skillfully beneath the arm of his own chair. It had been toying with something there for several long minutes. She would not have chosen that moment to relax into the softness of the divan, stretching and letting her legs come apart, spreading them slightly as if in seductive invitation. Her eyes were blinded by hunger, but in the instant before he pushed one of three barely-hidden buttons, she did begin to understand what was to happen to her.

Any other woman would have been foolish to make herself

comfortable in Gustav's house. But Jenna would have been foolish not to, for as the sound of compressed air hissed at four points around her, she felt the familiar sensation of being placed expertly into bondage against her will—and yet, her will was to be placed in bondage—before she could protest. Never had she been restrained so fast—usually Gustav had savored her captivity, undressing her slowly, wrestling her feebly squirming body into position, binding her wrists and ankles to the bed or the sofa or the legs of a table with slow, methodical torment.

Now, he had no time for such games.

The arms of the divan had burst with the speed of explosive bolts. Flexible metal bands had closed around her wrists and locked into place, holding her immobile. Each leg of the divan had four similar devices—for she now saw that the divan was split down the middle, into two separate legs. She saw this from the way the metal bands around her ankles and lower thighs drove firmly into locks placed with sharp edges that ripped into the upholstery. A matching band had gone around her waist, padded, fitting her smoothly as if she'd been built for it. The last restraint had been placed at the back of the headrest, and formed a stiff collar around Jenna's throat, holding her head in place. As she struggled, she felt fear heightening her arousal.

The divan was indeed a copy of a Chinese piece. In fact, Jenna now remembered, in a rush, having read about it in one of the tawdry paperbacks she had found moist and discarded in the trash near the waterfront. A paperback that purported to be "a serious academic study of restraint." The name it gave this particular style of chair was too horrible for Jenna to say, even now, with her humiliation at Gustav's hands once again imminent. But that was not because it frightened her, but because of the thunderbolt it sent through her body, electrifying her between her thighs as the brandy snifter went spinning out of her hand and shattered on the hardwood floor.

And in any event, Gustav said it for her.

"It's known as a rape chair," he said with pleasure, fingering the second of three buttons underneath the arm of his chair. "Quite a handy piece to have. But I dare say you're the first married woman who'll have the pleasure of experiencing it."

"Release me," said Jenna, her breath coming short not from fear but from sudden arousal. "Please." She had planned to toy with Gustav, to tease him, perhaps not even to sleep with him on this trip. She wanted to see him on his knees, to hear him begging for the chance to fuck her again. But now, the only begging was to be hers, and hearing the words come from her lips did nothing to dispel the heat that flared anew, now scalding, terrifying, between her slightly spread thighs.

"Please," she said, her nipples hardening even further as she said it.

"I don't think so," said Gustav. "You planned this when you came over here, though I imagine there was more cajolery on my part." Jenna reddened as she realized how well Gustav knew her. "There'll be no cajolery this time, Jenna," said Gustav. "It'll be just like the old days. You spread your legs, and I fuck you."

Gustav depressed the second button, and with the swift hum of an electric motor, the legs and arms of the divan slowly separated. The arms moved quickly, forcing her own arms up over her head in a smoothly-described arc. The legs, however, took their time, as Gustav had doubtless designed them to do—so that he could savor Jenna's slow, torturous humiliation. Jenna struggled against the tightness of her ankle restraints, her cunt throbbing with each strained twist of her leg muscles. Her thighs, too, were forced wide by the bands, forbidding even the slightest gesture of resistance on her part. She was trapped—imprisoned. There would be no seduction, no flattery, no inveiglement. Gustav would not attempt to get her drunk. He would not tease her about her need for him; she would not get to flirt with her ex-lover in the hopes that he would take her fiercely, as he had so many times before. There would be only a cruel fate Jenna had hungered for these past six months, with her husband's every halfhearted thrust into her.

Jenna's legs continued to part, forced open by the divan until the upholstery, strained to its limit, tore, revealing that the divan's padded frame was metal underneath, and its pivot point was at the small of Jenna's back, the padding underneath folding smoothly away so that both her sex and her ass would soon be fully exposed.

The divan's legs bent at the point of her knees, forcing her legs up into the air and allowing them to be spread still wider. So wide were her legs, in fact, that Jenna began to feel the strain of her muscles, the grind of her hip joints—she had become decidedly less flexible in recent months, having abandoned the Eastern disciplines that Gustav had instructed her in.

Gustav toyed with the second button as Jenna's legs were forced still wider, until the dress's slit, placed so suggestively between her thighs, was tormented to its limit. The thin fabric ripped to her navel, revealing the shaved slit of her sex between wide-open legs. Her legs were now open so far that she could barely move, her body twisted in an agonizing posture as she fought to thwart the cruel machine.

The divan hummed to a stop, and Gustav looked disappointed.

"That's as far as it goes," he said, his eyes roving hungrily over Jenna's exposed inner thighs. "I would have given it another six inches or so, but apparently the mechanical demands of the design forbid it. Luckily, I've more tricks up my sleeve."

Jenna gasped as Gustav depressed the third button, and the center of the divan began to rise, forcing Jenna's ass up high, bending her at the waist. Her upper half was now pointed down at a slight angle as the whole device rose to a predetermined height—a height Jenna could well imagine put her sex and mouth at the level of Gustav's cock.

Gustav stood and stroked the arm of his chair.

"Three buttons on the right," he said with glee. "And one on the left. I can release you all at once, you see."

"Please," whimpered Jenna, her ruined red dress all but falling off her. "Please, Gustav, press the button. You mustn't have me like this." Even as she said it, she knew he would not—and she prayed that he had not changed in the six months since he'd taken her. "I'm a married woman, now." Her cunt was pulsing with heat, hungry for his cock.

Gustav stood beside the divan, reaching between her forced-open legs. His hand slid smoothly under the tattered remains of her dress, touching her cunt. Jenna gasped at the pressure between her lips, and despite her show of resistance, found herself pressing against him. Two fingers disappeared inside her, and Jenna let out a low moan. Due to the infrequent plumbings she'd experienced since her marriage, Jenna's entry was quite snug, and the two fingers stretched her deliciously, causing the slightest hint of discomfort as Gustav penetrated her—not unlike the pain she'd felt when first being fathomed by his unusually large cock.

"Wet as an ocean, my dear," said Gustav, bringing his hand to her face and forcing his fingers between Jenna's full, lipstick-reddened lips. She fought not to accept his fingers, but she found she could not close her mouth. She tasted her own tang, ripe with fresh hunger, the familiar taste—so often experienced on the freshly-withdrawn shaft of Gustav's cock—sending a warmth through her body. Gustav withdrew his fingers and smeared her moistened lipstick over her face, making a tsking sound.

"Cocksucker red," he sighed. "How well I remember it.

You don't wear that shade for your husband, do you?"

"You're horrible," said Jenna feebly, fighting to keep her throbbing hunger from showing. She knew that if Gustav had any doubt that his treatment of her was deserved and desired, her gushing cunt had dispelled it. Nonetheless, she fought to maintain her resistance—if only because a torrent of guilt had just taken her over.

Gustav bent over and fished in the remains of the shattered brandy glass for a big enough shard. He plucked it delicately from the mass of splinters by what had been the rim, and brought the sharp fragment to the low *V* of Jenna's plunging neckline. Jenna quivered in fear as she felt the cold glass touching her skin, the sharp end nestling between her apple-sized breasts.

"No brassiere, as usual," said Gustav. "I've been appreciating the view since the moment you came in, but I believe it's time to reacquaint myself with those lovely tits of yours."

Jenna shivered to hear that word—she had always despised it, as she had disliked the other four-letter word Gustav used to describe her anatomy. But Gustav's repeated use of those words had always created that shiver, and a creeping sense of dirtiness that had never failed to make her do his bidding.

Jenna felt Gustav tugging at her dress with the shard of glass. He pulled until the neckline gave way and he was able to slit the dress down the front, its smooth slice joining with the ragged one started by the forcible spreading of Jenna's legs.

Now exposed down her front, Jenna felt the cool air of the parlor caressing her skin. Gustav reached up and with the shard of glass he made short work—almost no work, really—of the thin straps that held the dress on. Jenna moaned in despair, her cunt opening up with desire, as Gustav pulled the remains of the ruined dress out from under her, even the expensive silk giving her tender buttocks and firm shoulder blades what amounted to a rope burn. Jenna could feel the heat at those vulnerable points, her only contact with the divan, as if the pull of the dress from underneath her was needed to remind her that, except for the chain and locket that rested around her neck—the locket now tangled in her long dark hair—she was inexorably, inescapably naked.

Having rendered his captive helpless in her nudity, Gustav came around to her head, his crotch bulging with desire as his cock tented his silk robe. "One word," said Gustav as he reached for the sash. "I merely wish to hear you say it again, and then I'll let you go without plumbing that sweet body of yours. You know the word, Jenna. You've said it many times before. Say it once, and I'll even call you a cab."

Jenna struggled to speak, knowing that Gustav would be true to his word. She even had the *M* out, and was attempting the sound of the *er,* when Gustav opened his robe and brought his cock to her lips.

Part of Jenna truly intended to say the word. She even vainly strove to enunciate it after her mouth had opened to accept his cock, even after she felt the tightness of her collar around her neck as she strained to push the hard shaft, salty with pre-come, deep into her mouth, finding that she was so restrained she could not even properly give him head.

But the word did not come, and the slow thrust of Gustav's hips took care of the rest.

Jenna had not deep throated since her marriage. Lewis was a passive recipient of fellatio at best, and Jenna made a good show of being a respectable—that is to say, not too enthusiastic—fellatrix. Her throat proved tight against the thick head of Gustav's cock, which it had not done since he had first trained her. Nonetheless, Gustav showed no mercy. He thrust his cock down Jenna's throat and ignored her muffled whimper as her entrance was violated.

The feel of her old master's cock sliding down her throat sent a pulse of pleasure through Jenna's naked body that rendered her helpless. Gustav's hand came down between her legs as he leaned forward to fuck her, and the first touch of his fingers on her clit drove her past the point of no return.

"Ready as always, Lady Jennifer. I daresay you'll enjoy your first orgasm since your wedding night?"

The fear of that knowledge in Gustav's hands flooded through Jenna as she rose toward orgasm. Had he guessed it? Did he know her that well? Or was there some darker magic afoot? Had Gustav somehow plumbed her deepest thoughts and learned of her growing dissatisfaction with Lewis—her sexual needs outstripping the hunger for status and money that had led her into her marriage?

Then all was lost as Jenna's body exploded in white heat, orgasm taking her as her throat opened wide for Gustav's thrusting cock. "Deeper, deeper my dear," he growled as he shoved more firmly into Jenna's hungry body. "You're always a better cocksucker after an orgasm or two."

And another *was* coming—quick on the heels of her first, it took Jenna with a ferocity that made her cry out, only the stretch of her throat around Gustav's cock muffling the howl of this second—and, as usual, more intense—orgasm.

Gustav withdrew his cock with a shudder, pulling the swollen head from between Jenna's full lips. Jenna's lips followed it, her neck straining against the collar as her mouth sought to recapture the prominent organ. Gustav's long shaft hovered just out of reach, sticky with the scarlet of Lady Jennifer's ruined lipstick.

"Please," she whimpered, her tongue slipping, desperate, from between her quivering lips, her eyes wide, moist, and watery from the violation of her throat. It was how Gustav had always liked her eyes.

"Not yet," said Gustav. "Not until I've had your poor, neglected cunt. I see you've kept yourself shaved for me, Lady Jennifer. What does your husband think of that?"

"Please," gasped Jenna, her mouth working desperately to regain possession of Gustav's cock. "Please! Please let me suck your cock, Master."

"Tsk tsk," said Gustav. "With language like that, one might think you were down at the docks again, where I found you."

Jenna's mind could not process such an accusation. Instead, she whimpered desperately, her voice a hoarse whisper, "Fuck my face."

Gustav slapped her once, across her left cheek, bringing a sudden heat of humiliation to her. Restrained as she was, Jenna could not have gotten away from the blow even if she'd seen it coming. But she did see the second blow coming, across her right, and relished its impact as her cunt began to hunger for Gustav in earnest.

Gustav doffed his silk robe as he walked around her body, careful to avoid the shards of glass still scattered across the floor. He took his place between Jenna's spread legs and regarded her reddened, tear-stained face as she strained to lift her head so she could watch him enter her.

But the collar that held Jenna's head in place prevented her from seeing that moment of violation. Instead, she consented herself with looking into Gustav's eyes, seeing the cruelty that she had so craved as he prepared to take her.

Gustav smiled as his cock hovered between the swollen lips of Jenna's sex. "What's this?" He reached out and seized the locket from the tangled mass of her hair, pulling free a few strands as he did. Jenna cried out, feeling panic seize her.

"Still wearing your locket, my dear?" asked Gustav, yanking the chain unceremoniously so that it snapped. His cockhead rubbing at Jenna's entrance drove her mind into swirls of hunger, so that she could barely comprehend what was happening. Gustav popped open the locket and smiled. "I see you've replaced me," he said, deftly prying the photo of

Lewis out of the locket. "But you haven't replaced your key." He held up the tiny key and smiled as Jenna's panic raged in her mind, battling with the hunger for Gustav's cock.

"Could this be the key to that diary you keep by your bed?" he asked. "Certainly your husband would be scandalized if he knew what was inside. Or do you think he already knows?"

Gustav leaned forward, reaching under the divan—which made his cock rub more firmly against her sex. Jenna moaned and strove to lift her hips, sought desperately to push his cockhead further against her clitoris. But Gustav had found what he wanted, and as he brought it from its hiding place under the divan, he drew back, denying Jenna what she so desperately wanted. Instead, he held up a black leather-bound book, with her gold-embossed name on the cover. She panicked as Gustav smiled down at her.

"Wh-where did you get that?" she asked.

"From where you've always kept it," said Gustav, bringing the diary down between Jenna's spread thighs. "Next to the bed where you so faithfully service your husband, when what you want is to be a whore, bound and spread to a table, fucked just like this."

Gustav drew the diary back and brought it down on Jenna's sex, the heavy book sending a thud through her body as he spanked her. His next blows landed, glancing, first on one thigh and then on the other, causing a sting rather than a thud, and Jenna yelped as Gustav chuckled. Three more blows landed in rapid succession on Jenna's sex, and the weight of them brought the ache of her clitoris back to life. Gustav leaned forward, shoving the book under the small of Jenna's back, and as he did so, his cock met her sex again, drowning all her fear in the hunger to be fucked.

The metal lock on the book drove into Jenna's flesh as Gustav rested his body heavily upon her.

"Please," she asked. "Where did you get my diary?"

"Come, dear," sighed Gustav as he brought his lips to her tits, encircling her nipples with a rough bite. "It's useless without the locket. Oh, I seem to have gotten that, as well. It seems all your secrets are soon to be on display."

Jenna moaned as Gustav's mammoth cockhead spread her lips, violating her. With one smooth motion, Gustav took her cunt, not even pausing as he felt how tight she was. Jenna felt her body stretching to accommodate him, that first hint of discomfort giving way to shudders of pleasure.

Gustav's cock sank fully into her, opening up her sex with the savage thrusts that had burned in Jenna's memory from the last time she'd tasted them. Moaning, Jenna writhed against the divan as Gustav tucked the key under the hood of her clitoris, pressing its sharp edges against her. The feel of cold metal at her most sensitive spot was enough to drive Jenna toward her third orgasm, making her squirm and gasp as the pleasure reached the breaking point inside her. But one further violation would be visited upon her before she was allowed to come, and it was not one to which she was accustomed.

She felt Gustav's powerful thrusts stroking deep into her in the rhythm that spelled his imminent climax. But even through the haze of unbridled pleasure, she could feel the pressure at her rear entrance, Gustav's free hand parting her cheeks forcefully as another circlet of cold metal violated her. It was the locket. Gustav shoved it forcefully into Jenna's back door, making her cry out in dismay as he took, with her most treasured possession, that entrance he had never used in all their months of secret meetings. Jenna felt her ass opening up for the locket, as Gustav's cock pounded ruthlessly into her. She lifted her hips until the metal band around her waist drove painfully into her belly, savaging her with each violent thrust of her body.

Gustav came, his heat spilling deep inside her as he

laughed. The familiar feeling of that hot seed drove Jenna to her climax, her cries drowning out what she would have done well to listen for—the door of the parlor, opening.

It was without a doubt the most intense climax Gustav's cock had ever given her, and therefore the most powerful release of Jenna's young life. But even in the midst of her passion, Lady Jennifer heard the heavy footsteps, the glass crunching under booted feet. She saw the shadow over her only an instant before a firm hand seized her tear-stained face and a fresh cock violated her mouth.

This cock, familiar in its own way, opened up Jenna's throat anew and stifled the cries of orgasm before she had finished coming. Confusion overtaking her, along with the sudden and inexplicable hunger for this stranger's cock, she strained to get a view of him. But within a dozen or two dozen thrusts, she knew who it must be. Perhaps it was the taste of his cock, which she had experienced many times while feigning a lack of oral skill; perhaps it was the scent of his sex, which surrounded her and suffused her world as she swallowed him again and again, his thrusts proving more violent, even, than Gustav's.

Or, more likely, it was the taste of his seed, which exploded down her throat as a familiar groan sounded overhead, but rough this time where it had always before been tender. The taste of that seed was ripe, more pungent than Gustav's, less bewitching. And yet, where she had always before spit it out into a handkerchief—with whatever delicacy a Lady can muster after giving her husband a halfhearted blow job—she now gulped it hungrily, and would have done so even if his pounding thrusts had not forced her husband's cockhead so deep into her throat that no enthusiasm was needed on Lady Jennifer's part to swallow every drop of his seed.

Gustav drew his softening cock out of Jenna's sex and wiped it unceremoniously on her sweat-moist thighs.

As Jenna looked up, she felt shame suffusing her, knowing that those cold eyes that regarded her were eyes she'd looked into many times, thinking she had the upper hand. Now, Lewis knew everything—or he soon would.

Shivering with the aftereffects of her orgasm, Jenna felt a flood of relief. Lewis regarded her with the rough contempt she had come to know only in Gustav's eyes. And yet, she knew it was hers forevermore.

"You make quite a pretty picture, Lady Jennifer," growled Lewis. "A whore with ruined lipstick and tear-stained cheeks. Much prettier than the virginal maiden you've pretended to be."

Gustav reached under Jenna, removing the diary from where it rested beneath the small of her back.

"What do you say, cousin?" he asked, fitting the key into the lock on the diary, even as the locket itself remained deep inside Jenna's aching back door, broken gold chain dangling out to tickle her rear cheeks. "Shall we end our three-year charade? You've certainly earned your slave, enduring her little pretense of virtue for so long."

"C-cousin?" asked Jenna.

"Oh, many generations back," laughed Lewis. "The Braeburns and the Partridges are related, all right—but my branch has long since lost its title. It's a sordid story I'll be sure to tell you after we know every filthy story *you* have to tell. But I suspect your stories are even *more* sordid than anything the Braeburns have been able to conjure."

"So, cousin, what's it to be with your innocent bride, now that she knows the score? Shall we leave her bound while we read her confessions?"

Jenna pulled firmly against her bonds, as if to reassure herself that there was no way she could escape. Looking up into her husband's eyes, she saw the familiar look that she'd seen so many times in Gustav's eyes—the mixture of contempt and approval that could only be seen in a man who wanted exactly what Jenna had to offer.

Jenna felt her fear giving way to release, as Lewis caressed her sweat-soaked hair.

"I think my wife has a better suggestion," he growled. "Don't you, Jenna?"

Jenna took a deep breath and nodded as best she was able with the metal collar still restraining her.

"I'll read them to you," she said breathlessly.

Gustav disappeared from between her thighs; in an instant, Jenna heard the whirring of the divan and the click of the metal restraints retracting from around her neck, wrists, thighs, waist, and ankles.

Her husband helped her up.

She walked on unsteady legs to the armchair where Gustav sat, as Lewis took his place on the divan. The locket remained lodged deep in her ass, but Jenna knew it was not her place to remove it.

That privilege belonged to her husband, now.

Jenna looked at the floor, for once not feigning shyness. Gustav held out the diary, and when Jenna accepted it, he handed her the key.

"By all means," said Gustav. "Entertain us."

Her hands shaking, Jenna fitted the key into the lock.

Fire and Ice

Rachel Kramer Bussel

Her hair is in pigtails, short ones that look beyond adorable. On an older girl, this wouldn't work, but on this twenty-two year old they strike the right balance between cuteness and flirtation. She looks just young enough that I get a slight chill, wondering if the six years between us signal my (or her) utter corruption. But she is an adult and she sits surveying the party crowd, cigarette in hand. She's the cohost of the party but looks as if she's waiting for it to be over so she can crawl into bed with her smoke and her stare. While she's waiting, I check her out surreptitiously. I know she's mature enough to do justice to my fantasies, the ones she clearly wants to provoke with her short black denim skirt, patterned fishnets, and skimpy V-necked white T-shirt with black bra peeking out underneath, perfectly trashy. Her intense stare darts out from the mess of disheveled hair she constantly pushes from her face, the better to hide from the world, though really she is the type of girl who desperately wants to be seen. You don't dress like that to be ignored.

We've met before, but you could call us strangers and

totally get away with it. I know enough details to find her the most fascinating girl in the room, a bundle of contradictions I'm dying to unravel. Otherwise, this party doesn't have much going for it; what had seemed like a fun night out has devolved into a crowd full of strangers, tired drinks, canned music: fun-by-numbers, but it's still better than watching the same old videos at home. And she makes it worth every idle minute of sipping my drink and trying to look lost in thought or at least casually busy. I stick around, knowing she's the kind of girl who likes to be kept waiting, even if *she* doesn't know it yet.

Her skirt falls to mid-thigh, which immediately makes me want to get under it. She's looking around with that calm, icy assurance that belies her years, but it's not that typical New York swagger, that do-I-have-somewhere-else-to-be/is-there-anyone-important-here-for-me-to-talk-to? look. I wonder where she culled her party guests, or maybe they're all her roommate's because nobody's paying her any attention, abiding the invisible *Steer Clear* on her forehead. I can sense the hesitancy as she takes each drag, fingers shaking infinitesimally, not wanting to admit to anything but her self-imposed bravado. That bravado is what I long to crack. In my head, I press my hand up against her eager cunt; make her buckle underneath me, claw at the wall, drop her cigarette and her façade as she succumbs to what she truly wants.

Looking at her all cool and calm, a vision comes to me—her, naked, on her hands and knees on a bed, her clit sparkling with the silver sparkling hoop surely dangling from its hood, her wetness so palpable I can feel it before I even touch it. Me, ready to fuck her, my hands tingling with arousal, my pussy jumping like it's been touched by a violet wand. I squirm as I fight off the urge to touch myself, to do anything to offset the almost agonizing arousal that has overtaken me with this fantasy, and with that surge I know that I'll have to overcome any lingering nerves and go up to her. Just as I begin to stride toward her, I see her walking toward me, and I fix my gaze on her, not smiling, not frowning, not giving anything away.

She halts in front of me, so close we are almost touching, and holds her cigarette up to my lips for a puff. Normally, I'm not a smoker and can't stand the smell, but from her the tobacco is somehow erotically charged, and I inhale and then slowly let it out, plucking the cigarette from her fingers and stubbing it out before pulling her head in for a kiss. Her lips are soft and hot and moist, and I slowly, sensually devour her mouth. I could spend all day like this, and instead of the frantic groping I'd anticipated, I move slowly, my tongue gently parting her lips and deliberately teasing and tickling, coating her teeth and then moving back to her tongue and luscious lips. Being so close to her mouth is making my pussy spasm again, hurrying me along when I would prefer to take my time. Her skin is hot, almost burning up, and I know that her pussy will be too. I tease her, toying with her tongue, sliding it between my teeth, biting her lips, small, sharp nibbles that leave her wanting more. I want her to pant for me, beg for me, lose all sense of control as she squirms in her stockings, no longer giving a damn what any of the overgrown hipsters here think about her.

Memories of her surface, in that magically convenient way they do, coaxed forth not with the deepest of thought but by the logic of the unconscious. I recall other parties, restaurants, where I've seen her idly playing with the candles, her finger darting into the flame, flirting with the heat to get to the wax, which she swirls around her finger, poking it into the wet, warm morass and then coating her hands with its flaky whiteness. I observed this for a while, the casual way she didn't flinch as she poked at the wax, her utter concentration as she went about her solitary task. I have never even been able to draw my finger through the palest part of the flame, the heat scaring me off even though I know it will not actually burn me if I move quickly enough. Just the hint of that danger excites me, and I know exactly what I will do to her once I get her alone.

I excuse myself and head for the kitchen, the tension between us suddenly too much for me. It's a welcome break, one I know she's not used to—once she has you in her clutches, you're usually trapped, but she doesn't really want the upper hand, just gets it by default most of the time and doesn't know how to get rid of it. This time, she won't have a choice. I feel the same familiar energy coursing through my blood, the kind that tells me I am about to do something that will change my life profoundly. It's not so much arousal as intense excitement, and I'm not all that surprised when she follows me into the kitchen, standing there silently as I pour myself another soda. When I turn around, she's surveying me intently with those dark, smoky eyes, rimmed in black but shining brightly at me, seeking something that I hope I can deliver. They are issuing a challenge, and I put down my cup, knowing that I have no choice but to take her up on it. I walk closer to her, also silent; the first one to talk will clearly lose this game, and I need to have the upper hand. I reach behind me and fish an ice cube out of my drink, then bring it to her lips, letting the icy droplets fall onto her neck and chest, drip down into her luscious cleavage. She opens her mouth and I slide it in, hearing it crack with the sharpness of her teeth.

While she bites, I do what I've been wanting to do all night, bringing my hand up under that skirt and pressing against the fire I find there. I push against her wetness, palpable even through the thin layer of clothing, my arm tilted so the edge of my wrist presses against her, not caring who might walk in; fucking the party host has its privileges. I move away slightly and then bring my hand back, nudging her, tapping against her, forcing her to react. She bites down again, splintering the ice, grinding her teeth as I'm now grinding into her. I bring one of her hands up above her head and the other quickly follows, and when I look in her eyes they tell me all I need to know. She is mine, wholly, completely, just like that, and that look melts me. I have to catch myself, force myself to stand up straight rather than sink down to the ground, pulling her with me. Instead, I push my body flush with hers, biting her chilled bottom lip, licking along its plumpness. I bring my knee between her legs and feel her sink down against me, needing as much contact as she can get, her pussy aching. I nudge her with my knee, then shove it hard against her and she whimpers, her nails digging into the wall, and then just when she's dying for it, I pull my knee away. I turn her around so she is facing the wall, her gorgeously beckoning ass sticking out, the skirt sending the most heated of siren calls. I leave it in place for now and bring my hand back, spanking first one cheek and then the other. The impact is dulled by the layers of clothing but this is meant only as a tease. In between smacks, I bring my hand back between her legs and push hard against her cunt, practically pushing the fabric up into her, and I can hear her breath hissing out. I pinch her pussy lips lightly, then her clit, wanting to tear off her tights and touch her for real just as much as she wants me to, but I go back to spanking her, and she leans her head against the wall, no longer certain what she wants or needs, too overcome to do anything but stick her ass out and let me decide.

When it's too much for either of us to take—we've become a cloying, writhing mass—we make our way into the bedroom. Candles dot the room, some in modest little glass votives, some big and bold enough to stand on their own. I push her down onto the bed and dim the one lamp, and we are surrounded by darkness, with only the flickering flames to guide us. She moans quietly and stretches her arms above her head, catlike, making it easy for me to lift her skimpy shirt and push her skirt down around her ankles. I tear at the tights, the rip of the fabric ringing through the air, leaving her naked lips exposed. Of course, she's the kind of girl who doesn't wear panties, who thinks that's a cool, sexy statement, only I have a hunch nobody's ever exposed her in quite such a way. I pull the tights off her and lean forward to bind her wrists with the webbed rags, and as I do she thrashes and moans louder, clearly in a different kind of heaven than the one she'd imagined. Every stroke of my fingers along her skin, whether a light, easy fingertip over her bicep, or the pinch of a hardened nipple, makes her pant even more. She is struggling, frantic, needy, combative, but with me rather than against me.

I couldn't walk away now if I wanted to, the force of her lust would surely overpower me in a second. Her struggle is only with herself; with her need to strain and stretch, to feel the shivers that wrack her body as the fabric presses against that thinnest of skin on her wrists, as it sends tickles up through her arms, as I complement those gentle skin taunts with bites along her arm, her stomach, her thighs. I'm scraping, biting, stroking everywhere except her famished cunt, which she pushes at me, begging me to finally, finally fuck her like I've promised to all night, promised with my pinches and smacks, my kisses and clawings. But it's too much fun to watch her squirm, to watch her try to get a word out; even a short one like "Yes" or "Please" simply becomes a ragged rush of air, a sigh, a moan, a clench. I stroke the backs of my fingers along her slit, so wet I almost slide inside against my will. Her feet try to kick off the skirt, but I *tsk* at her and she stops, moving within the limited confines the fabric allows, her legs only permitted slight room to part.

Maintaining the silence, I keep my eyes on her as I walk across the room, picking up a small white candle whose flame arches into the air. I walk back, my hand cupped in front of it to further the fire. She stills now, slightly uncertain, not sure if she truly wants this particular fantasy to come true anymore, but damned if she does, damned if she doesn't, because the need is so clear in her eyes it could burn me hotter than this candle. I tilt it slightly, letting a few drips spatter her belly, and she jerks but keeps those cool dark eyes on me. I continue, splashing droplets of wax here and there along her torso, darting along the path between her sumptuous breasts, rubbing the wax into her once it has fallen. She is so still now, her body on high alert for danger, for pleasure, for anything that will ease the fire between her legs. I hold the candle still in my right hand and shove two fingers deep into her pussy, with no warning, and now she lets out a cry, a scream of arousal and frustration, of pent-up need, of everything she has contained for far longer than the length of this party. I push further, then pull out and enter her again, her body easily navigable. I have to fight to control myself, to not throw the candle on the ground and myself on top of her.

There will be time for that later, but for now I go slowly, slower than either of us wants. Delayed gratification is highly underrated. I want to keep her on edge until she is ready to explode into a million tiny bursts of pleasure that leap from her body, coursing out in an orgasm worthy of a fireworks display, all bright light and loud boom, obliterating everything else in sight. I keep my touch light, stroking, teasing, feeling, rather than ramming my fingers in the way I might do another time. I get to know her every curve, every lingering stroke telling me something new. I feel each simple shudder, each reaction, a slow fizz that builds and builds. I pour more wax, watching the way it melts within the holder, the hot liquid swimming. I watch it harden on her and touch the residue, her skin slowly cooling beneath it. She looks up at me with glossy, wet eyes, filled with unshed tears of need and joy and fulfillment, eyes that have probably not cried in front of someone else in longer than she can remember. I pull my fingers out, paint their wetness along her leg and move up to kiss her. I kiss her hard now, strong and furious, wanting to push the tears back in, strike them from the record, give them to someone else. She is so fragile inside, and I don't need words to tell me that this is more than a simple fuck to her, more than a one-night stand with some older woman she'll later brag about to her friends.

"I'll be right back," I tell her, needing a moment away. In the hallway I feel like I need my own cigarette, but instead rush to the kitchen, not wanting to leave her for more than a few moments. I hurriedly fill a cup with ice, keeping it behind my back as I enter the room. Those eyes watch me so fiercely I almost want to blush; if I didn't know better, I'd say they see right through me. She's a sexual sci-fi heroine whose power lies squarely in her pussy.

"Close your eyes," I tell her, and her obedience is more powerful than a blindfold, a tacit trust placed solely in me. Power can't exist in a vacuum, it only feeds off the need for others to respect it, and I feel it surge through my body, keeping me safe and alive, needed and needy. Again I hold a candle over her, moving lower down her stomach, letting the wax drip near but not onto her cunt, teasing her with the heat's potential to sear as well as soothe. While the candle is hovering so close she can feel the heat without the actual wax, I fish out an ice cube and trace it along her tender slit and smile softly to myself as she arches her back and lets out a squeak. Her hand moves to sneak down toward me but can't, and I watch as the reality of her immobility passes through her brain. She wants to protest even though she knows she likes it, the body's instinctive urge to push away anything that might be threatening. But even if her hands hadn't been tied, I think she would have inched forward and then become still as she does now, her teeth gritted and eyes slammed shut as she arches against the dripping ice I keep rubbing along her sweet skin before shoving it inside her and watching as the icy water dribbles out of her. As I shove the frozen cube inside, I let a drop of wax fall on her lower stomach. The combination of fire and ice prove too much for her, and while I work the cube into her deepest hiding places, she comes, clenching my fingers, pushing the cube out of her, letting out a roaring scream that has been building for who knows how long. She shivers from the chill, from the orgasm, from the all the intensity I've just wrung from her, and I watch as she comes back down to earth, her face momentarily slack, at peace, no longer with any façade to maintain. I hold her down by her bound wrists for a moment, letting her feel my weight, my power, letting her know that I want to be in charge of her again, but will let her go for now.

I untie the knot and let her wriggle free, then blow out the candle and place it on the ground, allowing her to relax in her postclimax haze. I trail my icy fingers along her arm, teasing her with the lingering cold. She shivers and I pull her close, wrap her up in my arms. We huddle there, candles blazing around us, our bodies hot where our skin meets, cool where the breeze hits. She's still an enigma to me, but I've gotten a little closer to her core, and even if that's the closest I ever get, it will be enough.

The Super

Alison Tyler

His wife-beater T-shirt caught my eye first. The tight-ribbed cotton showed off his muscular arms and broad chest. I turned slightly to look at him, my hand on the small copper mailbox key, my whole body still like a deer considering the chances of crossing the street safely. If he noticed me, would that be a good thing or a bad thing? The connection happened suddenly. His eyes made forceful contact with my legs, and I felt each moment as he took his time appraising my outfit: slim, short skirt in classic Burberry "Nova" plaid, opaque black stockings, shiny patent leather penny loafers, and lace shirt with a Johnny collar that was probably a bit too sheer for work, but I'd paired it with a skimpy peach-colored camisole and nobody said anything. Maybe somebody should have.

He did.

"Wore that to the office today, did you?"

I blushed, instantly, automatically, and pretended there was dire importance in the action of checking my mail. My fingers felt the slippery multitude of magazines and catalogs stuffed inside the tiny box, and I hoped I wouldn't drop the whole handful of mail. I could feel him moving closer, and now I could smell him, as well. Some masculine scent, mentholated shaving cream or aftershave. Not cologne. Wouldn't be his style. No metrosexual, he.

His hands were on me now, thick fingers smoothing the collar of the shirt, then caressing the nape of my neck, his thumb running up and down until I leaned my head back against his large hand. Crazy, right? In the lobby of the apartment building, letting this man touch me. But I couldn't help myself.

"A little slutty," he said, "don't you think?"

My mind reeled at the insult. Slutty? The entire outfit cost more than a thousand dollars. The skirt alone was worth nearly half of that, and I'd gone without small pleasures for months in order to justify the expenditure. Now, his hand became a fist around my hair, gathering my black-cherry curls into a makeshift ponytail and holding me tight.

"Don't you think?" he repeated, his voice tighter, as tight as his fist around my long hair. With his free hand, he pushed my mail back into the box and flipped the door shut. I dropped my hands to my sides, no longer needing to pretend to busy myself.

"Yes," I murmured, agreeing suddenly. It *was* slutty, the skirt far too short for a professional woman, the shirt sheer enough to be lingerie. The whole outfit was much more appropriate for bedroom games than office politics. What had I been thinking when I'd dressed myself that morning?

"Yes—" he repeated, his voice tighter still.

"Yes, Sir," came just automatically in agreement, as automatically as my feet began to move when he pushed me forward to my apartment at the end of the long, narrow hallway. I stumbled once on the blue-and-maroon-colored Oriental runner, but he caught me, his other hand high up on my arm, so firmly gripping me that I could feel the indents of his fingers digging into my skin. I'd have marks; I could see them, dark eggplant-purple bruises showing each place his fingers made contact, but now I said nothing.

He hurried me through the door to the living room, then kicked the door closed and hauled me quickly to the sofa. I saw everything swirling around me. The chocolate leather of the sofa, the bare shiny wood of the floor. He sat down and looked at me, and I shifted uncomfortably before him. I knew better than to sit, knew better than to do anything but wait. Yet waiting was the worst. Waiting and wondering. And hoping.

Of course, hoping—

"Dressed like a naughty little schoolgirl," he hissed through his teeth. "Dressed in public like that," he continued, shaking his head now, as if he couldn't fucking believe it.

I looked down at my feet, head bowed, curls falling free now around my face, and all I could see were my polished loafers and his scuffed work boots, the dark denim blue of his Levis, the wood floor that I cared for with a special wax....

"Do you have anything to say for yourself?" he asked. "Anything to say in your defense?" I shook my head no. Immediately, he was standing, his hand around my hair again, my face pulled fiercely back so that I was looking up into his gaze. The way he held my hair hurt now, and I clearly understood the message he was sending me.

"No, *Sir*—" I said, quickly, but not quickly enough. He had me bent over the side of the sofa in an instant, my skirt roughly pulled up to reveal the lilac rosettes adorning the tops of my garters, then yanked even higher to show my black satin panties. I heard the sinuous movement of his belt as he pulled it free from the loops of his jeans, and then I felt the air—that crackle-shiver of moving air—before the leather connected with my upturned ass.

Fire. That was the instant vision alive in my brain. Fire.

Pain like fire, so hot and hard that I gasped for breath. The pain seemed to grow, spreading through me, flowing over me. He struck me six times with the belt over my panties before sliding his meaty fingers under the waistband and pulling them down. I closed my eyes now, knowing the pain would intensify without that filmy shield, and trying to prepare myself for this—even though I knew that was impossible. Nothing could prepare me for the way that belt felt against my skin. No planning. No pep talks. No inner dialogue. Each blow was new. Each stroke was alarming and satisfying, unending and irreversible.

"Say, 'Thank you, Sir,' after every blow," he commanded.

"Thank you—" I started, but he hadn't struck me yet.

His lips were against my ear as he hissed, "Are you messing with me, girl?"

"No, Sir!" Louder than I'd thought. Louder than I'd heard the words in my head. I sounded like a soldier. "No, Sir!" Punctuated fiercely with my inherent willingness to obey.

"Don't mess with me, young lady," he said, "don't test me," and then he kissed me, high up on my cheek, and I trembled even more. The feeling of his gentle lips pressed to me, combined with the knowledge that he was about to grant me a serious hiding, left me twisted and shuddering inside.

The thrashing continued, now with the belt meeting my bare ass, and I did my best to choke out, "Thank you, Sir," after each blow. Didn't do quite good enough, though, because he had to continually up the intensity of the blows to keep me in line. Until finally he moved forward, grabbed my arms, and used the belt to bind my wrists behind my back. Against the couch, I balanced, body arched, waiting, waiting for what came next.

I'd thought about this moment all day, and it had been difficult for me to get any work done. Every time I'd tried to concentrate, I envisioned myself with my knickers at my ankles, ass in the air, submitting to the punishment I so desperately craved. Needed. Yearned for. Deserved. Every time I opened a new file, or clicked my mouse on a spreadsheet, I lost myself in forbidden daydreams. Now, those daydreams were coming true. And as always reality left the daydreams in the dust.

I sighed, inwardly delighted, when he tested between my legs for the wetness. I felt as if only one stroke of his calloused thumb against my clit would get me off. But he didn't touch me the way I needed, changing my sighs to desperate mews.

"Not done, yet," he hissed at me. "Not quite done, yet—"

Before I fully understood what he was doing, he had me over his lap, my wrists still captured, head turned on a velvety throw cushion, my body in perfect position for a bare-handed spanking on my naked behind. I was already smarting, so hot from the belt, but that didn't stop him from delivering another series of stinging blows on my throbbing ass.

I squirmed my hips against his knees to gain the contact I craved, and this time, he didn't admonish me. He let me leave a wet spot on his slacks before undoing the buckle of his belt, freeing my wrists, and repositioning me over the edge of the sofa. This is the way he was going to fuck me, with my ass so hot and red from the belt and his hand, with my pussy swimming in sex juices.

He slid in and I gripped him immediately, and then he placed one hand in between the sofa and my body and began to stroke and tickle my clit as he fucked me. The sensations were almost too powerful to handle. I closed my eyes and thought about how I'd spent my day. From the second I woke up, still in bed when I planned my outfit, I'd thought of this moment. At work, when he'd called to check and see if I had been a good girl or a bad girl, I'd nearly lost it—hurrying to the bathroom to rub and rub at my clit, but unable to make myself come without the pain that he so generously dispenses.

The pain and the pleasure.

Now, as I came, I thought about our arrangement. Whenever I wear my schoolgirl skirt out of the house, I know I'm going to get a spanking, know that I'm going to have to be taught a lesson when I get home. That my man will have left his expensive suit hanging in the closet and changed into the working-class superintendent of our building, ready to dole out punishment to any needy young lady. Truth is, I can hardly get through a week without wearing something that will catch his eye and make him shake his head.

"I love it when you wear that skirt, baby—" Landon said.

I smiled as I looked down at the rumpled Burberry plaid, then imagined what I might sneak out of the house in tomorrow....

About the Authors

RACHEL KRAMER BUSSEL (www.rachelkramerbussel.com) is senior editor at *Penthouse Variations*, a contributing editor at *Penthouse*, and writes the "Lusty Lady" column in the *Village Voice*. She is the editor of *Naughty Spanking Stories from A to Z* and *Cheeky: Essays on Spanking and Being Spanked*, and coeditor of *Up All Night: Adventures in Lesbian Sex*, with several more dirty books on the way. Her writing has been published in over sixty erotic anthologies, including *Best American Erotica 2004*, as well as publications such as *AVN*, *Bust*, *Curve*, *Diva*, *Girlfriends*, Gothamist.com, *On Our Backs*, Oxygen.com, *Penthouse*, *Punk Planet*, *Rockrgrl*, the *San Francisco Chronicle*, and *Velvetpark*.

M. CHRISTIAN's work can be seen in *Best American Erotica*, *Best Gay Erotica*, *Best Lesbian Erotica*, *Best Transgendered Erotica*, *Best Bondage Erotica*, *Best Fetish Erotica*, *Friction*, and over one hundred and fifty other anthologies, magazines, and websites. He's the editor of over a dozen anthologies, including *Best S/M Erotica*, *Love Under Foot* (with Greg

Wharton), *Bad Boys* (with Paul Willis), *The Burning Pen*, and *Guilty Pleasures*. He's the author of four collections: the Lambda-nominated *Dirty Words* (gay erotica), *Speaking Parts* (lesbian erotica), *Filthy* (more gay erotica), and *The Bachelor Machine* (science fiction erotica). For more information, check out www.mchristian.com.

JOLIE DU PRÉ's erotica has appeared on the Internet, including *Scarlet Letters* and the galleries of the Erotica Readers and Writers Association. Her story "Itching for It" can be found at Extasy Books. Her work also appears in print in *Hot & Bothered 4* and in *Down & Dirty Volume 2*.

SHANNA GERMAIN splits her time between writing articles, drinking mochas, and doing "research" for her newest erotic stories. Her work has appeared in dozens of publications and anthologies, including *Clean Sheets, Heat Wave*, *The Many Joys of Sex Toys*, and Salon.com. You can see more of her and her work online at www.shannagermain.com.

Believing that a little bit of bondage goes a long way, **DEBRA HYDE** writes about delightfully kinky sex practices as much as possible. Currently, you can find her short fiction in *Naughty Spanking Stories A to Z, Dykes on Bikes, The Mammoth Book of Best New Erotica, Best of the Best Women's Erotica,* and *Best S/M Erotica 2*. An opinionated sexinista, Debra writes the long-running weblog, *Pursed Lips,* and invites you to visit her there.

JOY JAMES is a writer who divides her time between New York City and Washington, DC. Her erotica has appeared in numerous print anthologies and websites. Her very best writing, she claims, comes while laced tight in a Victorian corset. She can be reached at joyce.james@att.net.

MARILYN JAYE LEWIS's erotic short stories and novellas have been widely anthologized in the United States and Europe. Her erotic romance novels include *When Hearts Collide, In the Secret Hours,* and *When the Night Stood Still.* She is the editor of a number of erotic short-story anthologies, including *Stirring Up a Storm.* Upcoming novels include *Twilight of the Immortal, Killing on Mercy Road,* and *Freak Parade.*

ELAINE MILLER is a Vancouver leatherdyke who spends her time playing, learning, educating, performing, and writing. Her work has appeared in *Skin Deep II, Brazen Femme,* five of the *Best Lesbian Erotica* series since 1998, *On Our Backs, Paramour, Anything That Moves, The No SafeWord Anthology,* and quite a few tawdry porn sites. Elaine has a regular column in both *Xtra West* newspaper and *Desire,* the new Canadian lesbian magazine. www.elainemiller.com.

N. T. MORLEY is the author of more than a dozen published novels of dominance and submission, including *The Parlor, The Limousine, The Circle, The Nightclub, The Appointment,* and the trilogies *The Library, The Castle,* and *The Office.* Morley has also edited two anthologies, *MASTER* and *slave.*

BILL NOBLE's accolades range from reader selection as author of one of the *Best American Erotica* "Stories of the Decade" and a Pushcart Prize nomination, to the National Looking Glass Award for Poetry. He is the longtime fiction editor at www.cleansheets.com. He apologizes, with a slight, crooked grin, to the friends and lovers so capriciously disguised in "Her Beautiful Long Black Overcoat."

IAN PHILIPS (www.ianphilips.com) is a loud and proud sodomite, gentleman sadist, and witch-about-town. He's the author of two literotica collections: *Satyriasis* and *See Dick*

Deconstruct. He lives in San Francisco—where else?—writing and spanking away the day with his partner in all crimes against nature, including publishing, Greg Wharton.

TOM PICCIRILLI is the author of thirteen novels, including *A Choir of Ill Children*, *November Mourns*, *Grave Men*, and *Coffin Blues*. He's published over one hundred and fifty stories in the horror, mystery, fantasy, and erotica fields. Learn more about his work at www.tompiccirilli.com.

AYRE RILEY has written for *Down & Dirty*, *Naughty Stories from A to Z Volumes 3 & 4,* and *Master/Slave*. She currently resides in Hollywood, Florida.

THOMAS S. ROCHE's more than three hundred published short stories and three hundred published articles have appeared in a wide variety of magazines, anthologies, and websites. In addition, his ten published books include *His* and *Hers,* two books of erotica coauthored with Alison Tyler, as well as three volumes of the *Noirotica* series. He has recently taken up erotic photography, which he showcases at his website, www.skidroche.com. After a lucky thirteen years in San Francisco, he recently relocated to New Orleans.

SAVANNAH STEPHENS SMITH has a degree in anthropology and is a secretary by day and writer by night (and occasionally during her lunch hour). Life doesn't always turn out like one plans. Her work has appeared online at *Clean Sheets, Scarlet Letters,* and other web destinations, as well as in print anthologies. She finds it hard to resist chocolate, good whiskey, and buying more books. She struggles to quit smoking, but can't resist smoldering a little.

RAKELLE VALENCIA has jumped into the smut-writing business with both booted feet. She has stories most recently published and upcoming in *Best Lesbian Erotica 2004 & 2005, Best of Best Lesbian Erotica 2, Hot Lesbian Erotica, Ride 'em Cowboy, On Our Backs, Naughty Spanking Stories from A to Z, Down and Dirty Volume 3, The Good Parts, Best Lesbian Love Stories 2005,* and *Ultimate Lesbian Erotica 2005* to stack on the shelves beside her articles on natural horsemanship. With Sacchi Green she is coeditor of the anthology *Rode Hard, Put Away Wet: Lesbian Cowboy Erotica,* and she is editing the forthcoming *Dykes on Bikes: Short Story Erotica.*

SASKIA WALKER is a British author who has had short erotic fiction published on both sides of the pond. You can find her work in *Seductions: Tales of Erotic Persuasion, Sugar and Spice, More Wicked Words, Wicked Words 5 & 8, Naughty Stories from A to Z Volume 3, Naked Erotica, Taboo: Forbidden Fantasies for Couples, Three-Way,* and *Sextopia.* She also writes erotic romance for Red Sage Publishing and her first novella, *Summer Lightning,* will be available soon. Please visit www.saskiawalker.co.uk for all the latest news.

GREG WHARTON is the author of *Johnny Was & Other Tall Tales* and the editor of numerous anthologies, including *I Do/I Don't: Queers on Marriage* and *Sodom & Me: Queers on Fundamentalism* (both coedited with husband Ian Philips). Wharton was included in *Out* magazine's "Out 100" top success stories for 2004. He lives in San Francisco with his brilliant and sexy husband, a cat named Chloe, and a lot of books.

About the Editor

Called "a trollop with a laptop" by the *East Bay Express*, ALISON TYLER is naughty and she knows it. Over the past decade, Ms. Tyler has written more than fifteen explicit novels including *Learning to Love It*, *Strictly Confidential*, *Sweet Thing*, *Sticky Fingers*, and *Something About Workmen* (all published by Black Lace), and *Rumors* (Cheek). Her novels have been translated into Japanese, Dutch, German, Norwegian, and Spanish. Her stories have appeared in anthologies including *Sweet Life* and *Sweet Life 2; Taboo; Best Women's Erotica 2002, 2003,* and *2005; Best of Best Women's Erotica; Best Fetish Erotica;* and *Best Lesbian Erotica 1996* (all published by Cleis); and in *Wicked Words 4, 5, 6, 8* & *10* (Black Lace), as well as in *Playgirl* magazine. She is the editor of *Batteries Not Included* (Diva); *Heat Wave*, *Best Bondage Erotica*, and *Three-Way* (all from Cleis Press); and the *Naughty Stories from A to Z* series, the *Down & Dirty* series, *Naked Erotica*, and *Juicy Erotica* (all from Pretty Things Press). Please visit www.prettythingspress.com.

Ms. Tyler, a dabbler in all sorts of bondage games, remains ever faithful to her partner of ten years—and to a simple pair of stainless-steel handcuffs.

The pain passes, but the beauty remains.

—PIERRE-AUGUSTE RENOIR

Bestselling Erotica for Couples

Expertly crafted, explicit stories of couples who try out their number one sexual fantasies—with explosive results. Sure to keep you up past bedtime.

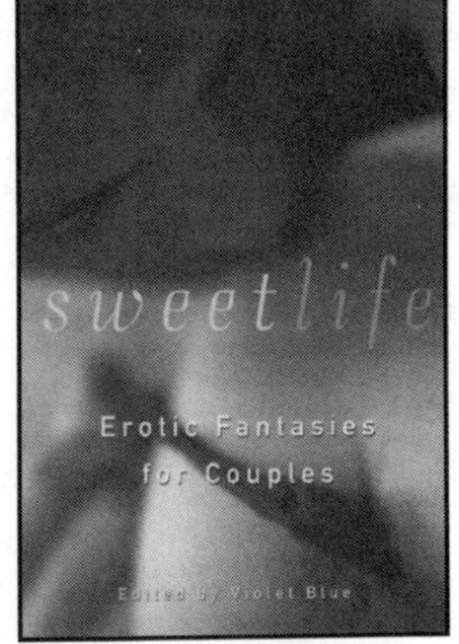

Sweet Life
Erotic Fantasies for Couples
Edited by Violet Blue
Your ticket to a front row seat for first-time spankings, breathtaking role-playing scenes, sex parties, women who strap it on and men who love to take it, not to mention threesomes of every combination…
ISBN 1-57344-133-3 $14.95

Sweet Life 2
Erotic Fantasies for Couples
Edited by Violet Blue
ISBN 1-57344-167-8 $14.95

Taboo
Forbidden Fantasies for Couples
Edited by Violet Blue
ISBN 1-57344-186-4 $14.95
What is *your* deepest, darkest, sweetest, most stunningly wicked fantasy? *Taboo* will feed you erotic stories of forbidden desire like fingerfuls of warm chocolate dripping onto your tongue. Superbly written erotic stories featuring couples who want it so bad they can taste it—and they do, making their most taboo erotic fantasies come true.

*** Free book of equal or lesser value. Shipping and applicable sales tax extra.**
Cleis Press • (800) 780-2279 • orders@cleispress.com
www.cleispress.com

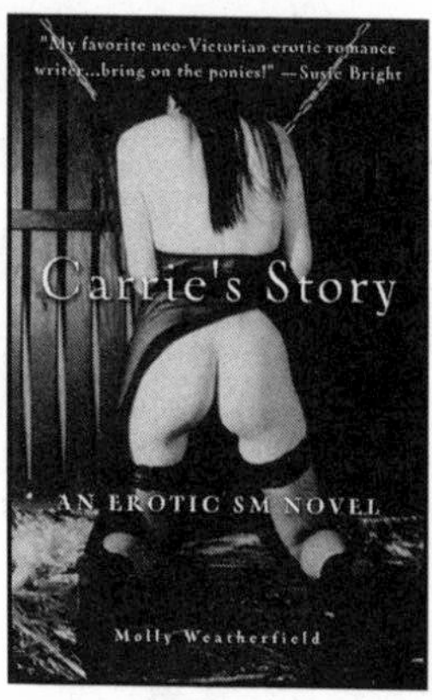

Bestselling Erotica for Adventurous Readers

Carrie's Story
An Erotic S/M Novel
by Molly Weatherfield
ISBN 1-57344-156-2 $12.95

"I had been Jonathan's slave for about a year when he told me he wanted to sell me at an auction. I wasn't in any condition to respond when he told me this..." So begins Carrie's tale of uncompromising sexual adventure. Imagine the *Story of O* starring a Berkeley PhD (who moonlights as a bike messenger) with a penchant for irony, self-analysis, and anal sex. Set in San Francisco and the Napa Valley, *Carrie's Story* takes the reader into the netherworld of slave auctions, training regimes, and human "ponies" preening for dressage competitions.

Safe Word
An Erotic S/M Novel
by Molly Weatherfield
ISBN 1-57344-168-6 $12.95

The sequel to *Carrie's Story*. Whisked away to Greece, Carrie learns new, more rigorous methods of sexual satisfaction. When her year of training is complete, she faces a decision—life on her own or in the embrace of a beloved Master...

Boy in the Middle
Erotic Fiction
by Patrick Califia
ISBN 1-57344-218-6 $14.95

How I Adore You
Erotic Stories
by Mark Pritchard
ISBN 1-57344-129-5 $14.95

Too Beautiful & Other Stories
Erotic Stories
by Mark Pritchard
ISBN 1-57344-138-4 $14.95

*** Free book of equal or lesser value. Shipping and applicable sales tax extra.**
Cleis Press • (800) 780-2279 • orders@cleispress.com
www.cleispress.com

Ordering is easy! Call us toll free to place your MC/VISA order or mail the order form below with payment to: Cleis Press, PO Box 14697, San Francisco CA 94114.

ORDER FORM

Buy 4 books, Get 1 *FREE**

QTY	TITLE	PRICE

SUBTOTAL	
SHIPPING	
SALES TAX	
TOTAL	

Add $3.95 postage/handling for the first book ordered and $1.00 for each additional book. Outside North America, please contact us for shipping rates. California residents add 8.5% sales tax. Payment in U.S. dollars only.

*** Free book of equal or lesser value. Shipping and applicable sales tax extra.**

Cleis Press • (800) 780-2279 • orders@cleispress.com

www.cleispress.com

You'll find more great books on our website